THE GOLDBERG VARIATIONS

THE GOLDBERG VARIATIONS

NANCY HUSTON

McArthur & Company
Toronto

This paperback edition printed in Canada by McArthur & Company in 2008

McArthur & Company
322 King St. West, Suite 402
Toronto, ON
M5V 1J2
www.mcarthur-co.com

Library and Archives Canada Cataloguing in Publication

Huston, Nancy, 1953- [Variations Goldberg. English]
The Goldberg variations / Nancy Huston.

Translation of: Les variations Goldberg. ISBN 978-1-55278-755-7

I. Title.
PS8565.U8255V3713 2008   C843'.54   C2008-905149-1

Printed in Canada by Webcom

The publisher would like to acknowledge the financial support of the
Government of Canada through the Book Publishing Industry Development
Program (BPIDP) and the Canada Council for our publishing activities. The
publisher further wishes to acknowledge the financial support of the Ontario
Arts Council for our publishing program.

10 9 8 7 6 5 4 3 2 1

To him who met the death of a child.

You have exactly ninety-six minutes.

You have all the time in the world.

ARIA: BASSO CONTINUO

Liliane Kulainn

Now it has started and there's no stopping it, no way of turning back. A space of time has opened; I'm the one who
opened it and now I must see it through to its close. From
now on I'm at the mercy of this time, I no longer have the
choice, I must travel with it to the end. An hour and a half,
possibly a shade more. Not anything like an hour and a half
of sleep, or conversation, or teaching; I'm not allowed to turn
around and smile at the others in the room, though among
them are people I have loved and still do love; I must think
of nothing but my fingers—and not even really think of
them; if I do I know they'll turn into gobbets of flesh, pale
sausages, wriggling little piglets, and I'd be liable to break off,
horrified to see them rolling about on the bits of ivory.

I've taken off my watch—it bothers me when I play. My
hands must be wholly given over to the ritual; *during this
time*, the constraints of performance must be absolute. Like
when there is a conference and they glue headphones to my
ears and I have to translate for four hours straight. In each
case someone else's message passes through my body. In each
case my task is to interpret rather than create. But when it's

words that penetrate my ears, get processed by my brain and re-emerge from my mouth in another tongue, I can hesitate, correct myself, stammer, even make grammatical mistakes and the content will still remain the same. Here, the content is the form—the slightest slip damages the message, sullies the clarity of its meaning—so every single second can be judged. Worst of all is that, for the entire duration of the trial, I have no access to the music itself. I'm here to bring it forth and they are here to absorb it, but the music blossoms in an intermediary space that touches neither them nor me. In fact I'm executing, not interpreting. The music must be put to death. I am the executioner of the immortal.

Spots are scattered across the surface of a page: whole notes, half-notes, quavers and crotchets. They were arranged in precisely this pattern, two centuries ago, by a gentleman who wore a powdered wig and had a great many children. One day he covered the pages with spots and they were printed by a publisher, reproduced by another and then several more, until they took on the form of what I have in front of me right now. My eyes register this form and transmit its image to my brain, which in turn conveys signals to the muscles of my shoulders, arms, and pale sausages, all of which respond at once, moving to carry out its orders. Before me stands the instrument—but the instrument of what? A musical instrument, they call it—but am I not myself the instrument of the music? In order to play, one needs to understand—and I understand next to nothing of what is going on. When words are involved, at least I know

I'm dealing with a given number of units endowed with a relatively stable value. I can predict how, when combined in such and such a manner ("hunger," "the Third World," "the population explosion"), they will tend to elicit a particular emotion, after having entered the ears of those present and stimulated certain regions of their brains. But a note of music has no meaning whatsoever. A higher note? A lower one? Both at once? Are you moved now? Shall we add a bit of rhythm? How about a repeat? Is that better—are your eyes beginning to smart?

Here, no one is weeping and no one will. Chamber music wasn't conceived for that purpose. People come together, dressed more or less in their Sunday best, to witness the unfolding of a ritual. Corrida in G major. But what is it they hope to feel? And what do I myself feel?

I feel nothing. That, in fact, is the prerequisite. When I set out to learn a piece of music, I turn it into a separate tactile thing, with a shape I can grasp in my hands. In the end, it's no longer a question of listening at all; my ears serve only to criticize the dance of the white piglets. Feeling has been supplanted by knowledge.

And yet I remember having felt—really felt something for the harpsichord. Love at first sight. I was thirteen and piddling around at the piano. A revolting instrument. Its true name is not the piano but the pianoforte. The soft-loud. First soft, then loud. *Crescendo. Diminuendo.* Then very very very loud, fortissimo. Then put the audience to sleep for a while with a moderate dynamic, *mezzo piano* or *mezzo forte*. Then startle them awake with a violent *sforzando*. Lead them by the nose through the whole gamut of intensities: feel this, feel that, do you understand? It's like a man screaming! It's like a bird chirping! It's like the ocean rocking you and drifting you to Never-never land! It's like, it's like, it's like.

With the harpsichord, "it's like" does not come into the picture. The harpsichord simply *is*. Or rather—when I heard it quite by accident for the first time—*that's* it. The harpsichord doesn't make music express things; it allows the music to express itself. Instead of hammers, it has dampers—and even they are covered with felt. I'd wake up in the middle of the night, with my parents in the room next door. Daddy would be yelling and Mummy would be crying—or else Mummy would be yelling and Daddy would be crying. I would cringe and huddle up beneath the sheets. Then diminuendo down to sobs, then low murmurs of reconciliation, and then silence. That's emotion for you. That's the pianoforte. It's revolting. With the harpsichord, everything is a matter of register. If I decide the repeat should take the form of an echo, I pull a stop and everything hushes at the same time. I can *control* the coupling. I can't make the instrument cry out by using violence. We are profoundly in agreement, perfectly in tune with one another—at least on that score.

Once, a vision of an ideal instrument came to me. In a sort of waking dream, I entered a huge room, silent and empty, and there it was, looking like a harpsichord except that it was perfectly square. It was made of gleaming black wood. The keyboard seemed to invite me to touch it. I sat

down on the stool, in a state of anticipation I've never experienced in real life, both curious and absolutely calm. I
played the E above middle-C. A crystal-clear E rang out, as
though I'd blown into the glass flute of Dionysos. The note
hovered in the air, I allowed it to evaporate, and, enchanted,
I played it once again. And then the E an octave higher…
only it wasn't higher than the first, it was identical. Not a different perfection, the same one. I could scarcely breathe. I
played the G-sharp and the B between the two E's—they,
too, were E's. Both of them, all three, all four of them were
as one. The whole instrument was tuned to the same note:
all its strings were of exactly the same length; no matter
where I placed my hand, only the E rang forth. In a state of
indescribable rapture, I began to play scales of E's at top
speed—all the major and minor scales my fingers had been
running up and down for thirty years—and what came out
was not the same, it was the same, it had a full and perfect
sameness. At last, I decided to take my revenge on the 19th-
century composers whose insipid and grandiloquent sonatas
I'd been forced to learn: I played them one after the other on
this sublime instrument, which gathered all their poor passions together into a single point. My fingers flew across the
keyboard in a veritable orgy of purity, an orgy of precision.

But today is different. Today I have a trial to endure. The
public, however private, bears witness at this trial. And I
know very well that, deep down, the harpsichord is an instrument of torture. Trial by music: this is the wheel to which I'm
strapped. Will I be able to withstand the tension for a full

hour and a half? That is what they're wondering as they purse their lips, wipe their noses, cross and then uncross their legs. A human body—alive, present, fallible—has sat down in front of a few sheets of music. The question is whether or not this body will wander off the path traced by the pages. For this music is transcendent—it existed before I was born and will continue to exist after my death. Today, of my own volition, I'm grappling with it. Yet "it" is just as much a victim as I am, because "it" is not simply these pages covered with little black spots. The real music depends on me for its existence. I can splinter it, I can crack it, I can smash it to bits... and I don't want to. So the two of us struggle *together*, in the world's most delicate wrestling match. This particular combination of sounds is like a huge and fragile chandelier tinkling beneath my fingers: if I make the least false move I shall break a piece of it; if I slow down at the wrong moment its brilliance will be dulled. I am carrying the chandelier—which is a burden not because of its weight but because of its weightlessness, its absolutely tenuous nature—for I am carrying it through time, not through space.

Do these people consider music a pastime?

Do they consider it a waste of time?

And do they realize they're growing older as they listen to me play?

VARIATIO I: SHADOW

Adrienne

Following. Just beside. Just behind—once again. As usual. Helping the other little girls dress because I wasn't cute enough to play a daffodil. "Adrienne's so clever with her hands—quite a little seamstress!" I can sew, yes—other people's costumes—and tie ribbons into the curls of their blonde hair, and little do they care if I, too, want to dance. So they're right: I don't want to anymore. But music…that, they'll never take away from me. Even if I can give myself up to it only in private, almost in hiding. Music is my solitary vice. My nerves would never be strong enough to exhibit it in public. Even now, I'm more nervous than Liliane. My hands are trembling; hers aren't. Panicking—and they have so little to do—though they're intimately familiar with *The Goldberg Variations*, having caressed the most secret and inaccessible reaches of this music.

My heart beats madly, while the artist remains serene. The instructions she gave me were straightforward: for slow movements turn one bar before the end of the page; for the fast movements, two bars. As for repeats… Well, Madame insists on preserving her spontaneity. She does not wish to decide in advance which of the variations she will repeat and which she won't. She cannot even tell me (each variation being made up of two parts) whether the first half will be repeated and not the second or vice versa. I am therefore obliged to *watch* her, to see whether she will nod her head at the critical moment—and then, in a flash, remove my buttocks from the chair, extend my left hand (*above* the music, not in front of it), seize the top right-hand corner (and only the corner) of the opposite page, and draw it back towards me, *prestissimo* but without a sound. If the paper rustles, it will be my fault; I shall have spoiled the music... But that's not the worst thing that could happen. What if I unintentionally turned *two pages* instead of one? Of course, Liliane knows the music well enough not to stop playing at once. But then I'd have to make amends, and everyone would notice my discomfiture. They'd know I was the one who had committed the *faux pas*. They'd think it must have been a Freudian slip, an accidentally-on-purpose act of sabotage designed to ridicule a woman I'm jealous of.

But there's no reason for that to happen—we've rehearsed together dozens of times and it never has—so I'd better not provoke the accident by thinking about it. On the other hand, it might very well happen that I get lost. It would only take a moment's inattention, Liliane's fingers would carry on without me, and when she reached the end of the page I'd still be trying desperately to catch up and force my eyes to see what my ears were hearing. Or else, at the other extreme, I might get carried away by the beauty of

the music and stop paying attention to its actual performance—imagine it accelerating, as it were, and turn the page
too soon. Liliane would toss her head frantically—"Not yet!
Not yet!" or else "Come on, turn!"—and I'd be sitting there
like an idiot, trying to come back down to earth and figure
out where she was.

So. I must pay attention. Even more closely than Liliane.
Her body is the miraculous passageway through which the
thing called music flows. All she has to do is allow it to pass
through her, and she will be borne aloft upon its waves—
whereas I am a hoppy little beastie at her side: one!—turn
forward, right this second, two!—turn back for the repeat—
and so on and so forth. Forever following. Forever just
behind. Artists need inferior creatures like myself. Like the
Greek and Roman sculptors made famous by the Venuses
for which their courtesan mistresses had been the models.
Okay, so I'm no model. But wasn't it similar when I was
working for Bernald? Adrienne's nimble fingers once again.
He had the ideas, and I snipped them into shape. His mind
would go out and perform its acrobatics in public, and I
would dress it up, decorating it with colourful ribbons so it
would seem beautiful and pleasing to everyone. I typed his
manuscripts to perfection: twenty-five lines of sixty-five letters each, or thirty lines of sixty letters, depending on the
publisher's specifications; the two of us worked together to
produce a clean and bright and shiny object, and when it
came out only Bernald's name was on the cover.

It's only natural. I'm not an artist. I used to adore what

Bernald wrote, just as I adore Bach. For me, sitting at a type-writer keyboard is the same as sitting at a piano keyboard. I'm incapable of invention; perhaps I have nothing to say. Which by no means implies that I don't understand what's going on. On the contrary, I understand everything. Sometimes even better than the artists themselves. Take Serino, for instance—he's here tonight—it's perfectly obvious that his life exists only with and with respect to music. He is nothing but a two-lunged shell, an *ersatz* of a human being. Now, *I* know what it's like to feel anxious and torn, so I can appreciate his music, whereas his own emotions are expended within the four walls of his studio. So why is the production of a work of art val-ued so much more highly than its reception? Artists are an egotistical, petty lot—most of them, at least. Look at Liliane. I'm sure she isn't even listening to what she's playing; her fin-gers move mechanically from one chord to the next. I, on the other hand, *love* what she is playing; I grasp every nuance, every modulation, every sigh of it. She plays a bit too rigidly for my taste—but she has decided once and for all: Bach was an anti-Romantic, his music is as pure as calculus, and it would be a betrayal to imbue it with sentiments he never intended to express. For each variation, she chooses a *tempo* and sticks to it from beginning to end. Never the least tender *rubato*; never an unexpected embellishment; the vibration of each trill is calculated to end precisely on the beat; and there you have it—your money's worth and not a penny more. Well, no…the concert is free and of course she does play well.

As for me, as soon as I sit down at either keyboard, I get

fatal temptations. I know both machines perfectly—but that's just what incites me to make mistakes. I get haunted by the possibility of disrupting the prescribed order. At the type-writer it's not too serious—I even enjoy rereading to see whether my typos are significant slips of the mental tongue; for example, it often happens that I type "greed" instead of "freed" because the F is right next to the G. But at the piano, slips are less amusing: it's impossible to go back and change a G into an F. Music is incorrigible. Either you play Beethoven's *Appassionata* Sonata or you don't. For months and months you practise it, writing in all the fingerings, mucking up the pages with pencilled figures and exclamation marks; a thousand times you go over the scale that descends in *accelerando*; you master it little by little until it truly does sound like a waterfall; you commit to memory each succes-sive section and the transitions between them, the articula-tion—and then—impossible to perform. There will always be a finger that defies me by crossing over the thumb a bit clumsily... Plonk! You can't just pretend nothing happened. Beethoven, deaf as he was, would have plugged his ears.

So I'll stay on the sidelines, I'll go on following and yearn-ing and failing just as I always have. Yes, I'm following you, my fair Liliane, as others have done in the past. Each toss of your head is an order I have no choice but to obey. Fortunately, you're not one of those pianists who toss their heads back and forth in paroxysms of musical pleasure. No, you are every bit as controlled as the way you play Bach. Apart from your beautiful white hands, your body is motionless.

Your feet are flat on the floor in front of your chair—luckily the harpsichord has no pedals to cause your legs to part, however slightly. Your back is as straight as I was always taught to hold mine—both in typing and piano lessons. Your stomach is sucked in—a real armature of muscles; a built-in corset.

No, I'm wrong—you are moving. I can see your teeth nibbling and chewing the flesh at one corner of your mouth. Those full pale lips must have some sensitivity after all, or you wouldn't need to punish them like that. Who would have believed it? Not once have I seen them parted in a hearty laugh—never more than an ironic smirk. Oh, Liliane, I simply can't forgive you. Go ahead and punish your own sensitivity if you must—but why Bernald's as well? Never shall I forgive you for that. You destroyed the one thing that gave meaning to my life—even if secretarial work is probably degrading in your opinion. It gave me as much joy to type his pages as to turn yours, Liliane. How did you manage it? What did you tell him? What threats did you use? I must be careful—keep my eyes glued to the music—or I'll start to scream in front of everyone. But do you realize what you've done? Deprived this city, this country, this language, of one of its most powerful and original voices. And then you have the nerve—whether out of cynicism or genuine indifference—to invite his acquaintances to your home and flaunt your musical talent in front of them. And I am given the honour of sitting right next to the star—well, no, just behind her, just barely concealed by her long, black dress—and popping up like a jack-in-the-box every time she nods her head—

VARIATIO II: WINDS

Jacques

…seem to be rather slow choices of *tempi*, but I don't mind. That way you can really hear every single note, which is rare. People have gotten so used to virtuosi that they expect to hear Bach played at top speed as if it were Chopin or Liszt, and pianists destroy the polyphony by insisting on the soprano line as though it were a melody, whereas the point is to try and listen to all the voices interdependently. You can tell she's practised them separately, one never loses the thread of what's going on in the left hand, or even in the middle voice which weaves back and forth from one hand to the other— you can hear it so clearly you'd think Liliane had a third hand emerging from her chest—and the effect isn't muddied by a pedal. To think people play Bach on the piano—how dare they? In the first place, the harmonies were different in his day, based on a slightly unequal temperament; so there are chords that sound like shit on the piano because the piano's intervals are false, which is to say equal; in the second place, anyone who'd play a piece like *The Goldberg Variations* on the piano could only be a showoff since it was written for two keyboards and the fingers necessarily get tangled every time there are crossed scales or arpeggios. So of course it's possible to voluntarily take on the extra technical difficulty and proceed to overcome it with brio, but it's not as though Bach hadn't made things difficult enough as it is. In fact some of the pieces virtually exist to illustrate a particular difficulty: a single hand playing a trill and a melody at the same time; broken chords played with alternating hands...maybe Bach wanted to put little Goldberg's talents to the test; in any case he was a brilliant pedagogue and Liliane has followed his lessons conscientiously.

But it hardly matters since no one ever listens to music anyway; that's why you have to sit in the front row if you don't want to be bothered by people picking their noses or smoothing their skirts or whispering to their spouses—"Are you sure you locked the door?" I should consider myself lucky nobody brought their kids along—they'd be sure to start whining in the middle of the most subtle passage. Honestly. Kids are nothing but a hassle, I can't understand why people keep having them, especially in our day and age, when everyone knows the planet's full to bursting as it is. I hope Myrna means it when she says she agrees with me on this, and won't let all her gossipy friends put ideas in her head, the joys of delivery and whatnot. She's started harping about what a drag it is to take the pill, she's been taking it for six years now and every so often she forgets, she says it's no fun swallowing chemicals every day and why don't I look into what's available for men? She's heard about these heated underpants guys can wear to cook their balls—honestly, how does she expect me to get a hard-on wearing a thing like that and if we decided to screw in the morning would I have to put it back on and for how long? Is it like a hard-boiled egg or a soft-boiled egg? No, she's got to be kidding. Seriously, though, she'd better not get pregnant. I can't see myself cleaning up the mess a baby would make if I left my study for five minutes, or going to concerts alone five nights a week and leaving Myrna at home to look after the kid. It's true old Johann Sebastian had a pile of them, twelve or fourteen or some such wild number, but I bet that just encouraged him to lock himself away all the more to write his music, so it was probably all for the best. After all, Bach's works turned out to be immortal and his kids didn't. There was that skit we saw in the café-théâtre, pretty funny, with Bach's wife pregnant to the teeth and trying to practise the cello and being constantly interrupted by little Karl-Friedrich or little Anna-Magdelena or one of the others. Anyway that's all over now. In our day and age you see women like Lili who are excellent musicians and manage to live a rich emotional life at the same time—she can't complain, even if she doesn't look completely happy, still a bit on the somber side, but not as somber as before, or she wouldn't be giving her first concert in years and living with Bernald Thorer, which is not so bad going. In fact what happened when they fell in love was the exact opposite of the traditional scheme of things, so she can't complain.

So what am I going to say in my article for *The Day*? It's always a bit pointless writing a review of a concert no one will be able to attend because it's already taken place, a concert that hasn't even been recorded—but even if it is pointless, Lili's an old friend and I don't mind doing her the favour. I wonder if she really intends to launch into a career as a concert harpsichordist at this late date, I rather doubt it, I think she prefers to lead the sort of life she's always led, the life of a delicate dilettante—supported, ironically enough, by UNESCO—a bit of theatre, a bit of music, a smattering of poetry and dance… Everything she does, she does well, but with a strange detachment, a lack of conviction, as though she were destroying what she built as she went along. It's always reminded me of that scene in *Five Easy Pieces* where Jack Nicholson goes home and sits down at the piano—to the intense satisfaction of his sister, who thinks the black sheep has at last rejoined the flock—he plays a Mozart *adagio*, she's so relieved there are tears running down her cheeks, and at the end he tells her flatly that he hasn't felt a thing, that playing the piano means nothing to him, absolutely nothing, and she's horrified at how cold he is. Lili's a bit like that—a bit cold—not that cold, of course, but cold enough for Bach to suit her. Maybe I could call the article "Thirty Difficult Pieces"… No, I doubt people would get the joke, but what can you say about *The Goldberg Variations* that they don't already know? I could focus on the idea of chamber music, since she's purposely invited us to her bedchamber. This is where her harpsichord is and where she probably practises every day—a lovely room, too, you can tell it's hers, it's filled with a sort of lugubrious calm—especially the heavy purple bedspread, there's something funereal about it, that must be the bed she and Bernald Thorer make love in, I must say it's hard to picture, they're always so dignified and reserved and sort of sad, I wonder what it's like when they start horsing around, the imagination falters. But they do seem to be in love—in his case, anyway, it's obvious. Poor man—no, he doesn't look any worse off than before, so who can say?

Chamber music in a bedchamber, then—to recapture the spirit of intimacy prevalent in the eighteenth century when Bach's music was composed. Yes, that's it. There might even be a quasi-political paragraph, something along the lines of... "In our day and age, bombarded as we are by junk music from radios and loudspeakers, inundated by records of all kinds, hypnotised by the megashows of foreign orchestras and operas, benumbed by the deafening rhythms of punk and disco, what do we know of the subtle pleasures tasted by the music-lovers of yesteryear, who gathered to spend an evening among friends in appreciation of the great composers? Thanks to Liliane Kulainn we rediscovered that pleasure last night." Mm hm, not bad. Then I could go straight on to a brief historical description of the *Variations*, then say how painstakingly faithful Liliane was to the master, then maybe a sentence or two on the renaissance of the harpsichord in the latter half of the twentieth century, and that would be it.

Myrna isn't listening at all. She looks a thousand miles away, like she does sometimes when I'm talking to her and I suddenly realize she's been out of it for the past ten minutes... It's funny, though—she likes classical music; she was thrilled at the idea of coming here tonight. I know she would have preferred not to sit in the front row—she's so shy it makes her feel as if she herself were on stage—but after all, how am I supposed to talk about the artist's hands if I can't see them? Lili has lovely hands, her fingers are long and strong, and she holds them right next to the keys the way you have to on the harpsichord, there's no point attacking from above like on the piano, you'd only get a dull thud when the key struck against the wood. Harpsichord virtuosity can only be expressed through control, never through excess—that sentence might come in handy, too—

VARIATIO III: SCARLET

Myrna

If I keep my thighs squeezed really tight it won't come out. I read that in some countries adolescent girls learn to retain their menstrual flow, releasing it only when they pee. You shouldn't have worn a light-coloured skirt. Boy, are you dumb. But Jacques likes this dress, we bought it together last summer and I wanted to look good for him tonight. Does he give a damn about looking good for you? Look at his potbelly, do you think it bothers him? If I gained so much as half a pound I'd stop eating right away. You've made a good start on your diet, yes indeed, what with those scalloped potatoes you wolfed down at lunch and the cake just before the concert. As a matter of fact this dress is getting a bit tight around the waist, isn't it? Maybe I'm pregnant. Oh yes, of course, that must be why you're having your period. And the Pill, as everyone knows, was conceived to get women pregnant. No, you're not in the family way, it's nothing but plain old fat. You'll be really obese one of these days, no doubt about it. Jacques will keep the potbelly he acquired in his thirties and leave it at that, he won't get any worse. But women turn into saggy bags.

Liliane isn't sagging. I've never seen her as beautiful as she is tonight—all dressed in black, with her skin so white—she looks like something from a painting. Men never play the harpsichord in paintings, only women. Proper young ladies were instructed in the art of "touching" the harpsichord; it was considered appropriate to their fragile charms. They "touched" it rather than playing it. What did the little boys do while the little girls took sewing and harpsichord lessons? Perhaps they went hunting with falcons? I don't know. This isn't an exam; I don't even know what century we're talking about. When was the harpsichord invented? I must have known that once, but I don't remember. You forget everything. Bach, for instance—what century did he live in? Come on, I'm not asking you for his exact dates, just the century. It was a period when religion was very powerful in Europe, since most of his works were commissioned by the Church—"In Europe"? What does that mean? Germany? Austria?—so it must have been around the sixteenth or seventeenth century. I don't give a damn, anyway. That isn't the way I appreciate music. Who cares if everyone laughed the other day when I asked about the Beirut Festival? For me, music has nothing to do with erudition; it has to do with reverie. I could listen to a Mozart symphony fifty times without knowing what key it was in, whereas Jacques immediately pounces on the record cover: "Terrific! The C Minor!"—or whatever—"Who recorded it and when? Who's conducting? Ah! To think Mozart had just returned to Vienna, ill and penniless, and found the courage to write *that*!" So I'm forced to think about such details, and give my opinion on the orchestra—I say whatever comes into my head, but I'm so afraid of saying something dumb that I stop listening to the music. Or else you put that absent look on your face—as though the music had plunged you into a bottomless meditation—and don't answer the question at all. I feel so tense, so threatened. That's what you get for living with a music lover. But does Jacques really love music ?

There…I just felt some blood ooze out. Dammit. Couldn't you have changed it before the concert started? I don't know where the bathroom is in this house. After all, a drop of blood on a woman's dress isn't a catastrophe. When I was twelve years old, sure, it was a big deal, and I went home from school with scarlet cheeks in the middle of the day because of a spot on my pants… But people could get used to it, couldn't they? It's been happening once a month to half the human race for thousands of years, and they still react as though it were abnormal. On my temperature charts, they're called "sick days." Honestly. Pregnancy is classified as an illness, too, under my health insurance plan, whereas without it there wouldn't be any people, healthy or sick. If they want to get upset about blood, why don't they take a look at the battlefields? But that, of course, isn't an illness. That is nice, red, patriotic blood, they don't mind it at all, in fact the more the better, and if there isn't enough in the papers and on the TV news, they guzzle it down by the gallon in novels and movies!

…"Music for a While." There's a song by Purcell called "Music for a While." I think it's my favourite song in the whole world. I don't understand all the words. I don't speak English very well, but it's very slow and poignant and it says you have the right to think about nothing but music from time to time—not all the time but once in a while; you don't have to constantly be thinking about wars and domestic quarrels and money problems or whatever; you can simply close your eyes and open your ears and find bliss in music for the time being. The English word *while* is beautiful because its duration is indefinite: it means a certain length of time—which is to say an *uncertain* length of time, and that makes me want to cry because music-making and love-making are the only activities during which time itself is suspended and no longer counted; it just flows and I'm utterly given over to what is happening to me in its flow, the musical or sexual ecstasy—what a joke. Who do you think you're kidding? All it takes is for the upstairs neighbour to turn on the radio, and your interest in Jacques's body comes abruptly to a halt. And if there's so much as the slightest risk of ecstasy on the horizon, you immediately start thinking about the shopping you have to do tomorrow after work—would it be better to buy one or two packages of ground beef?—it all depends on the size of the tomatoes—anything, rather than sink into the pleasure that is making your innards vibrate and threatening to tear you away from your humdrum train of thought. As for "Music for a While"—that's a good one, too! What have you been thinking about since the beginning of this concert?

Your drenched tampons! Do you so much as know which variation she's playing right now? And you have the nerve to claim that *Goldberg* is one of your favourite compositions! Jacques, of course, will have been keeping track.

So let him keep track for me. I don't feel like it. If he can do a dozen things at once, good for him. It's like driving—he can wend his way through traffic and talk and smoke and whistle *Leporello* between his teeth…well, and I just can't, that's all! For me, it's clutch, gears, accelerator, rear-view mirror, blinker… The thing he just calls "driving" gets broken down into a multitude of disparate movements, and when he's there watching I find them virtually impossible to coordinate. It's incredible, I've had my license longer than he has, but he's the one who watches me and not the other way around. His lack of confidence in the way I drive implies I don't know how to lead my life, either. I get clumsier and clumsier. I keep thinking how all it would take is the tiniest jerk of my arm when I'm passing a truck on the highway for both of us to get killed. I grow more and more obsessed with the idea of making such a fatal gesture, more and more scared of making it unintentionally, I start to sweat… Even if everybody knows, statistically speaking, that women have fewer accidents than men, the image of the "woman driver" is there between us; it refuses to budge. And there's no doubt but that women do drive differently from men. I remember one day near the Arc de Triomphe, I saw a woman bus driver trying to make it through a yellow light. It turned red when she was smack in the middle of the intersection, and cars started coming at her from three directions at once. A man in that position would just have honked his horn and cursed, and the other drivers would have let him through. But this woman, I'll never forget her, she just folded her arms on the steering-wheel and laid her head down on them. Despair. We're always so willing to give up, plead guilty, blame ourselves for everything—

Come on now, let's not get carried away. Whenever you find the slightest little example, you turn it into an allegory for the Condition of Women in general. You yourself may lack confidence, but that's no reason to think it's a congenital deficiency of your sex. Take Liliane—does she look as if she lacks confidence? She's perfectly sure of what she's playing, she knows it's beautiful, she knows it gives her friends pleasure, it's as simple as that.

Once I asked her if she thought there was a meaning to life and she said no—meaning would imply that life was moving along in a particular direction, progressing for example from point A to point B to point C and so on, whereas she had always felt compelled to return to the starting-point again and again; nothing was ever ascertainable once and for all, and therefore life did not have one a *priori* meaning but many *a posteriori* ones. Something like that. Not an infinite but an indefinite number of them. And she laughed. I was grateful to her for talking to me like that— and especially for not finding my question stupid; it's the kind of thing I could never ask Jacques because he considers questions about the meaning of life meaningless in and of themselves: there are beautiful things in life and it's worth getting to know them; that's all there is to it; why do you have to bury your nose in a newspaper and take in all the horrors of the world—for all the good it does you—honestly, you never so much as open your mouth when there's a political discussion going on, it's as if you'd never even heard of gulags or ayatollahs, you only ingest current events, like music, to feed your fuzzy-edged reverie—just as you ingest food into your fuzzy-edged body...

VARIATIO IV: SIGHS

Pupil of Liliane's

...in fact, they're filled with panic. The sunset as they entered the same deep purple as Madame Kulainn's bedspread. Occident: where the sun is put to death. Suspension between day and night, suspension between variations, hiatus. This is the most beautiful of all. But people flee from silence. They dread it. Anything but that. "A deathly silence," they call it. Like a trap door they might fall through, a pit that might swallow up their "identity." They can't stand it. Have to keep on proving they are someone. Using words.

During lessons, we almost never spoke. She understands. That music is built on silence. A bridge across it. We once spent an hour on a single bar of Frescobaldi. The first note resounds. The second comes to join it. The two mingle there in the air, you hold on to them, weaving in an *arpeggio* with the left hand and allowing the whole thing to reverberate together, you remove one finger at a time, the chord is transformed, unravelled bit by bit, the silence is reconstructed and finally becomes whole again. What do they know about *fermatas*, hesitations, springers and suspensions—all that goes into making up the breath of music, its invisible aura?

Nothing. They know nothing about anything. They don't want to know. Give us this day our daily noise. Fill us up. Madame Kulainn used to say: before you begin to play, you need at least a full minute of silence. To build on. Otherwise it won't be solid. That's what she taught Monsieur Thorer, too. Everyone's upset. They just can't understand. Why should he have ceased pouring his wisdom into our ears? Heaven help us: he's gone dumb! That isn't true, of course. I know why this concert is being held. To force people to shut up.

You bring them together in the same room and they jerk their gregariousness into gear. They want—they need—to babble; rub their lips together and say me, me, me. But music forces them to wait. After all, they do respect conventions. They know they're in the presence of great art. Their tongues are condemned to inertia. They'll start up again right after-wards, of course—that is, after barbarically destroying all the accumulated silence by clapping. Even at the age of four, I found it outrageous. My mother and I were in the kitchen making pastry; there was a string quartet on the radio. I clambered onto a stool and gazed at the radio, glassy-eyed, seeing nothing. The piece came to an end. The silence was complete. I felt jubilant. Then, all at once, a terrifying racket ripped the air to pieces. I ran to my mother. "What's the matter, dear?" *"What is it?"* "Oh, that's just the applause. It means the people really enjoyed the music." I've never believed that.

At least concerts accomplish that much—they make people temporarily hold their tongues. Other art forms don't. Books don't count—you're alone when you read, anyway. At movies you're together, but the word machine is running full tilt. But take that away—stand people in front of a painting, a sculpture, a pyramid—there's no helping it, they get logorrhea. I can't set foot in museums anymore; they're too grotesque. Visitors come in groups with a guide, some talky lady who feels the need to "contribute something to society" now that she's past the age of fifty. Or else they come in couples and it's worse. The husband has bought the catalogue at the entrance and reads it aloud for the edification of his wife. Or else the young man puts a scholarly expression on his face and says to his girlfriend, "Quite an *extraordinary* blue, wouldn't you agree?" Or whatever. All of them. They talk, and see nothing. Right now they hear nothing. But at least they have to keep their mouths shut. Only because of the rules that govern public concerts—not at home, of course. Instead of giving them access to silence, instead of marking out the path that leads there, music is used as a dam. Or as a "background." "Background music." Cocoon. Womb. Food. Cigarettes. You don't know what to do with your hands, so you light up a cigarette. Sometimes you get distracted and light up a second one a moment later; the first one hadn't caused your tension to drop enough. Same thing with music. You don't know what to do with your mind, you feel the great void approaching, so you turn on the radio. Sometimes you feel like turning it on again, whereas the background noise is already going full blast. You need a sort of background to the background. It's still not full enough, not totally dammed up. You're in a car with friends and suddenly there's nothing left to say. Quick—the radio! A bit of reggae, that'll bring us back together. We were on the verge of veering off into our private paranoias. Now we can tap our feet in unison, that proves we're on the same wavelength. Same thing with airports. Above all, don't feel anything. Separations, reunions, the abysses that can open up between relatives or lovers, moments of doubt or disarray—no, all that gets stuck back together with Vivaldi Glue, arranged for saxophone and electric organ, filtered through the Arrivals and Departures loudspeaker.

Same thing with films. Wherever there's a blank in the screenplay and the dialogue peters out, they have to add music to carry the action forward. Swelling of violins. Chitchat of percussion. Anything will do.

Madame Kulainn told me about a dirty movie she'd been to. One scene showed a naked woman being hunted down in a forest. The soundtrack was a Scarlatti harpsichord sonata, played with inimitable violence by Sonya Feldman—who had been Madame Kulainn's teacher for several years. Her world-famous name was duly mentioned in the credits at the end of the film. She wrote a letter to the producer and demanded it be withdrawn. The producer complied. But withdraw the Scarlatti sonata? Unthinkable! A young woman being hunted down in a forest—*in silence*?

Now it has gotten dark. There are candles everywhere. The house looks like a haunted castle this evening. I'm sure it was Madame Kulainn who wanted it that way. I know why she chose the *Variations*, too—because she's that way herself. In fragments. Even her poetry. She's never written anything but poetry. She told me once she'd like to write a book, and I was taken aback. But it was a book in which there would have been blank spaces wherever she'd hesitated before writing. For instance, if it took her ten seconds to write one line, then one minute's hesitation would be equivalent to six blank lines. And so forth. Whole pages would be blank—that way, readers would see that there was nothing self-evident about literary inspiration. Moreover, they themselves would be able to write whatever they wanted in the empty spaces, building either on the words preceding or on words of their own. Madame Kulainn laughed as she described her idea: it goes without saying that such a book would never sell. Such a waste of paper! But in *The Goldberg Variations*, at least there's a bit of breathing space between fragments. It's like a sigh...and the musician can change character during the pauses. Madame Kulainn sighs a great deal, I remember. She would sigh when I played well, and she would sigh when I played badly. I've never heard her speak five minutes without stopping. She usually pronounces a phrase and allows it to hang in the air, like that bar by Frescobaldi, waiting to see if someone else's *arpeggio* will come to join it, then tries another phrase—or lapses into silence.

I know that's what captivated Monsieur Thorer. Never had he seen anyone living at such close quarters with silence. Frequenting it like a friend. Cultivating it. His own life was composed entirely of words. Books, lectures, radio programs, interviews; every minute of his life, people solicited his wordy wisdom. And Monsieur Thorer wasn't the worst of those who live that way. Far from it. The public admired him all the more for being unpretentious. Having a soft, rather than a stentorian voice. Speaking in his own name, rather than propounding a theory. Claiming to prefer dialogue to dogma. Never had the public seen anyone so generous with his intelligence.

They threw themselves on Bernald Thorer as a ravenous dog throws itself on a bone. They sucked him dry. They spied on him in his favourite cafés. They borrowed his style and parodied it with affection. His hypotheses were virtually weightless. A hypothesis is something to spread beneath a thesis—like a net. Like a piece of music. He knew that his own were suspended in mid-air. But people used them just as they use music, to build bridges and dams. They appropriated his ideas in order to betray him.

This went on for years. Seminars, invitations, honours, celebrations of what Bernald Thorer could do with words. He treated them as something other than weapons. He was allergic to polemics. People had never seen anything like it. Attacked, he wouldn't even defend himself. A sort of Christ.

But a Christ with no Truth. A Christ without a Father in Heaven. They praised him to the skies just the same. They hallowed his name. And then, one day, the castle of cards collapsed.

He's here, tonight. I know he's listening, totally receptive to the silences of Madame Kulainn. I can feel it.

People wish he looked haggard. They wish he'd turned into a hermit—or, better still, committed suicide. That, they could have understood, it's the sort of thing you see every day—men who kill themselves for the love of a woman. A deathly silence. Bullet through the head. Blackout. *Finis.* Curtains. But to have him here among us, just sitting and listening to the music. Happy. At peace with himself. That's what they can't accept. You let people rest in peace once they're dead. Not before. He's broken the agreement. Betrayed their confidence. They thought he could be counted on. And then he went and did that. Everyone knows geniuses can break down. Be committed to mental asylums. Embark on boats to Africa. Undergo rest cures or lithium therapy. But *that.* Just to stop, serenely. At least he could have had the decency to leave Paris. Or change neighbourhoods. But no—he's right here. In our midst. Wearing the same smile. It's obscene.

She loves him. She's playing for him alone. They're alone together in this room, their bedroom. They're making love. They're not talking. This whole thing means nothing. It *is*, that's all. Nothing else. Nothing.

VARIATIO V: JOUAL

Dominique

No sense to it. All these high-falutin' folks get together, who do they think they're foolin'? One two three four five six all the way to thirty, when they reach thirty-one they'll have come full circle and they can all go back to bed and fall asleep. Can't hardly keep themselves from noddin' off as it is. That's why the chairs are so goddamn uncomfortable—make sure we won't go driftin' off to dreamland. It ain't fair, given that this music was written specially for the very purpose. 'Cause apparently old Mr. Goldberg was one hell of an insomniac. He's the one who asked big-shot Johnny Sebastian for a bit of melodic and harmonic sleepin' draught. Johnny said OK, but if I write out the prescription on the spot, you're gonna hafta pay the price. Goldberg said Tut, tut, Doctor Whosit, money is no object. So Bach, who was already blind as a bat at the time, scribbled out the music as fast as you can say how-dee-do. You take one variation every night of the month, you get your little chamber maid or who-ever to stir it up for you and pour it into your ears as long as necessary, and sweet dreams. So Goldberg said, A thousand thank-yous, Doctor Whosit, I'll just run along and try it out.

So the first day of the month he started out with the theme and it worked like a charm—out cold before the repeat. Second day, first variation. And so on, up to the thirtieth day of the month. Fan-tastic. In months with thirty-one days they'd play the theme over at the end, and then begin again. Which obviously meant he'd have to listen to it two nights in a row. But I've never been able to figure out how Sleepless Count Goldberg organized the month of February.

Sweet Christ. Can you believe folks take themselves so seriously? A bunch of guys and gals that claim to be intellectuals, paragons of Reason in the land of the Enlightenment, gettin' together at the end of the twentieth century, for a mystical *séance*? Concocted by Lady Medium, who filled the room with candles before enterin' her trance. Let us now communicate with the spirits of Time Past. Let us call forth poor old Bach by fiddlin' with his pieces. (They opened up Bach's coffin and there he was, bent over his music with an eraser in his hand, furiously rubbin' out notes. Hey, Johnny Sebastian! What the hell you doin'? Leave me alone, he answers, I'm decomposing.)

Ah...that wouldn't make these Frenchies laugh; they're too goddamn uptight. I mean there's gotta be *somethin'* sacred, you know what I mean? So what if we did kick God out the front door way before you backward cretins got around to it. He crawled back in the window in the form of art, and we've got the right to make all the BlueWhiteRed genuflections we feel like. Who cares if we don't know sweet fuck-all about music? We know it's good, for Chrissake! We

know this is one of the bloody summits of Western Civ!
…They really think they're the Virgin's titties.

Do they ever whistle while they work? Do they ever sing
together—apart from when they get soused on fifty bottles of
their fancy wine and start bellowin' out one of their sleazy
songs about how great it feels to be together, comrades, and
then whammo!—under the table. Do they teach their little
ones to pick out tunes on the piano, so they can liven up an
evening with a few folk songs? Not on your life. They'd rather
sprawl out in front of the idiot box and watch the Tall Blonde
shimmyin' in her sequins. They'd rather boast about how they
stood in line seven hours for a ticket to the Opera. Fu-uck.
Tonight, all of 'em are proud as peacocks to be in touch with
Good and Beauty and the rest of the world can go to hell.
Music is high-class escapism. It's even better than the movies.
'Cause in the first place there's nothin' to understand. You can
run off and pay a visit to your castles in Spain, and no one can
accuse you of not havin' paid attention. You can glue a serious
expression on your face, settle your limbs into position number fifty-two known as Aesthetic Beatitude, and then zoom
away into an hour of free fantasy, and bye-bye Bach. The
advantages of music don't stop there. 'Cause these folks are all
imbued with ideology. They can't just read a book or see a film
for the fun of it, with no ulterior motives. They gotta be able
to stick it into one of their pigeonholes: idealism, humanism,
manicheism, romanticism, realism, or whateverism. But
music—what a vacation! No way you can pin down the ideas
floatin' around in there. Music is odourless—like money,

accordin' to their proverb. Music doesn't stink of i-de-ology, so you get all the fun with none of the guilt. Don't bother wonderin' what sort of "isms" Bach had in his head. Sexism, Catholicism, nepotism, who gives a damn? What he wrote was a bunch of little circles goin' up and down, not a bunch of letters ABC. So it disappears into thin air. Escapes from history. Its conception is as immaculate as the Virgin Mary's. My ass.

I wouldn't even be here if it weren't for Christine; she used to play the flute with this Liliane. A long time ago, when she was livin' here in Paris. Duets—same as she plays with me. I could be jealous, but it ain't the same thing—the guitar and the harpsichord can't be rivals. Christine adapts herself to everyone. She wants to reach out to everyone. She keeps gettin' herself burned. She brings old ladies home with her when she sees them sprawled against garbage cans. She makes mango tea for them 'cause that's all she's got in the house. In Boston, she goes wanderin' round the Combat Zone tryin' to talk to the whores. They send her packin' and she feels hurt. In Montreal, she goes into taverns all alone in the middle of the night, they kick her out, women without escorts aren't allowed. She rings me up at four in the mornin', mad as hell. But darlin', you know about that law. Then she tells me this joke about two Quebec feminists who go into a tavern and sit down, the waiter comes over and says, I'm sorry ladies but we only serve men here, and they reply, That's fine, we'll take two! Then she starts laughin' like crazy and I get feelin' scared for her. Christine doesn't belong to this world. She can't keep her feet on the ground. Can't hold down a job. Last week she was workin' as a shorthand typist, one of those temporary jobs that's supposed to give you so much freedom, her boss said she was the best substitute secretary they'd ever had, and she burst into tears. She lacks perspective. I don't know how to help her. So I bring her to France, just to get it over with. I pay for her trip so she'll remember that the year she spent here studyin' wasn't paradise on earth. It helps to take little hops back in time now and then, to remind you how the Golden Age stank just as bad as what came after. Just like Bach. Then she starts draggin' me from one place to the other and I go along with her, OK, so this was your favourite cut-rate cafeteria, here's where you met that drunk who told you about his four marriages and said he was a better writer than Shakespeare, and yes, all right, I'll tag along tonight and sit in on your precious Liliane.

It's true she's not bad-looking, but those veins can't have honest-to-goodness red blood flowin' in 'em. Look at her forehead, look at the backs of her hands. Her veins are like icicles—I know ice when I see it. How can anyone be so cold? The music is like icicles, too. Real pretty, the way it glitters in the sun, but you gotta be careful not to touch it. After a while there ain't nothin' left but a bit of slush on the ground. They're all gonna walk around in the slush afterwards: what a mahvellous concert! Wasn't it, though? And what did you think of it, *cher ami*? How did you find the *cesura* between the staccato and the legato passages? A bit risqué, of course, but so masterfully brought off! And Liliane: I'd like you to meet my dear American friend, Christine. She's a flautist. How perfectly chahming! The next time it will be your turn to give a concert. Oh, you simply *must*!

And Christine will turn red as the wounds of Jesus, she'll look at me, grabbin' onto my eyes the way a little girl grabs onto her mommy's hand, searchin' madly for the right answer, the answer that'll prove she's got what the French call *esprit*. Not a word will come to her rescue—not in front of these people—I know her. A good thing, too. But afterwards, when we've slipped away, when we're alone together, she'll start the old refrain: "I'm a misfit, I don't know how to talk, they were all so nice, what's the matter with me? I'm fuckin' crazy, I wanna die, I wanna die, I can't even talk to Liliane anymore, after all she did for me when I was just a little zombie student of hers—" Then I'll have to calm her sobbin' and tell her No, no, we love you, everyone loves you, Christine, you didn't do anythin' wrong, they're the ones who're crazy, come on, let's go back to the hotel, I'll run you a hot bath and we can tell jokes together and tickle each other, we'll have a good laugh, just the two of us, you'll see. Come on, Christine.

All that because the Intelligentsia, as they call it, is the dumbest, meanest thing in God's Creation. I'd rather chew the rag with my folks anyday, listen to 'em talkin' about how the animals are doin' and how much the price of rope was hiked this year; I'd rather hear 'em tell me "You just sit right there while we whip somethin' up," and then my ma will start hummin' some tune from her childhood while she sets the table, even if it's some dumb ol' song like "Gentille Alouette" or whatever—I prefer that "Alouette" to all the Count Goldbergs in the world served up roasted on a golden platter. Then we'd all sit down to eat, and the little ones would start askin' "Paris? Paris?" with eyes round like saucers, and I'd tell 'em once and for all that Paris ain't worth it, the chairs are as hard as the True Cross and so are the Parisians, so help me God, it just ain't worth it. Then they'd laugh and we'd join hands round the table and say grace and everybody'd be glad I was back at home and so would I. With my ma's hand on my right and little brother's on my left, at last I'd feel like there was really—

VARIATIO VI: MEMORIES

Pierre

…her vomiting on the island. She wouldn't let me touch her because she felt too ugly. Every time she thought she was less than beautiful, love had to stop. And that was often. At those times she preferred to be alone, and her wish for solitude immediately turned into an attack—you, of course, never need to be alone, since you're totally dependent on others for your identity—I'd let her go. Sometimes she'd be gone all afternoon, wandering through the island hills and coming back with her legs scratched up like a little girl's, her hair mussed, and even a bit of colour in her cheeks. She liked to play the wild child, when in fact she hated being cut off from the city. That was my fault, too. She couldn't sleep. She'd crawl out of bed in the middle of the night and shinny up a tree to stare at the full moon, then she'd come back and tell me in a tragic tone of voice how false everything seemed—all of it, even the moon, malevolently false—as though the island, its beaches, its palm trees, its white villas and its moon had been put there for the express purpose of distracting her from the things that really counted.

What those things were, I could never quite figure out.

Making love counted while it was happening—for once her eyes would cease to be penetrating, cutting, and turn into limpid pools. Sometimes she'd weep and press me to her. Ten minutes later, with a cigarette between her lips, she could be making a speech about "possessiveness and jealousy in modern society." Ten years later, I remember the speeches better than the love-making. How amazing to be able to look at this woman, in whose body I came so many times, and be incapable of imagining her naked and abandoned. With Hélène it's different... Liliane has progressed farther and farther into everything that made her distant from me. Watching her now, I'm amazed at my own serenity. And she's found someone else to humour her.

As a matter of fact, I'm the one who introduced her to Bernald. I'd introduced her to dozens of "great men." She'd always say yes, that she was curious to meet them, and then at the end of the evening, when we were alone together, she'd light into me because the conversation had been too superficial. She never made the least effort to put people at ease. They were on the hot seat; she was the judge, the jury and the executioner. She'd use her muteness like a fortress, locking herself up in a sullen, disapproving silence; her expression would grow more and more lugubrious—and then her tongue would lash out. I ended up fearing her tongue, and it's impossible to desire something you fear. I had a nightmare in which I was gazing at her lips and bemoaning my inability to kiss them because of all the horrors they had uttered.

Our reconciliations were deadly.

I wanted to make her happy—now I think that was impossible. I took her to all the places that held meaning for me, and she accused me of manipulating her. I begged her to tell me what her own wishes were; she claimed she didn't have any. That was a lie—the worst lie of all.

Not as serene as all that.

Wasn't music her island? That was where I felt cut off, floundering far from all my points of reference. But even this she held against me—mockingly, almost gleefully. "You don't know how to just listen; you need to be told a story." For her, I would have put up with all the symphonies of Beethoven, in succession and in silence—but not those words. In her opinion, music (like everything else) was not a matter of taste but a matter of personal philosophy. Once she lit out at me: "Why do you like opera? Hm? Do you think it's a mere coincidence?" That was one of the phrases she'd picked up from psychoanalytic theory: "It is no mere coincidence that..." And I wound up blurting out a piece of nonsense—about how I couldn't hear the class struggle in instrumental music—and naturally she screamed with laughter.

That night I was impotent.

"I don't know why it upsets you so much. Making love doesn't have to entail penetration. Really, it doesn't matter."

We went on that way for a long time, making each other more and more miserable but unable to break up. Until the day she made a choice—against the cows.

It was at one of those futile colloquia held each spring in Normandy. Thomas was one of the organizers, and he'd invited us to come and stay a day or two. Wonderful mood. She felt beautiful, she'd lost weight, she was wearing a black scarf around her head and the rings beneath her eyes were not as marked as usual. Returning from an after-dinner walk, we found ourselves exactly halfway between two fat cows chewing their cuds and two great men palavering. Bernald Thorer and Simon Freeson. I observed ironically that this was typical of our situation—torn between the love of nature and the love of culture. She giggled. It must have been that very night she fell in love with Bernald Thorer.

He'd given a paper that afternoon, brilliant as usual. Liliane was nervous and distracted. She'd taken a seat next to the door and was chewing on a blade of grass picked from between the flagstones at her feet. After Bernald's talk there'd been an extremely unpleasant discussion—an elderly English gentleman with white sideburns kept asking naïve and arrogant questions, throwing the entire audience into consternation. As the gulf between them was clearly impossible to bridge, the session came to a clumsy close. That evening, however, a couple of dozen "intimates" got together to drink and chat in the small salon. Someone begged Bernald to play the piano and he gracefully consented. All of a sudden the Englishman appeared, waving a sheaf of piano duets. They sight-read a few pieces together and the discord between them vanished into thin air. It was quite amazing.

Liliane's eyes were shining. I think it was then.

What does it matter?

It took us two more years to separate. Once—at the very

beginning, when we were still in the enthrallment phase, sitting next to the fireplace at Mornay—she had burst into tears while listening to Prévert:

Et la vie sépare ceux qui s'aiment

tout doucement, sans faire de bruit…

She was feeling a sort of advance nostalgia for our love. After the separation, I heard the song by chance on a jukebox, and it hurt so badly I had to leave the café. Now it has no effect on me at all—Hélène plays the record from time to time, she's very fond of it, so it's taken on a different meaning. Same thing for Dylan: when I was a teenager, every one of his songs was associated with some powerful experience; I'd hear them even six months later and the shock of memory would be unbearable. As time goes by, though, the shock lessens. Now, twenty years later, nothing remains of the original sensation and all I can remember is the dimming of intensity.

"Twenty years later." I would never have believed it possible to pronounce those words. As a child, I found it outrageous that adults could talk calmly about "four or five years" —say something like "I lived in Marseilles for four or five years." They inhabited the same time as I did, they got up every morning and went to bed every night and ate three meals a day just as I did—how could they allow themselves to be smothered by this soft, amorphous, viscous time? Then I, too, gradually grew familiar with the squid. Now my hair is falling out and it actually worries me, just as it used to worry my father, and I no longer feel quite so chipper on mornings after nights before; I'm starting to "take care of myself" and to talk the way other people have always talked, as though the "self" one took care of were someone else, as though the body were a foreign body that had to be dealt with separately. And my brain contains images that elicit the words "twenty years later."

For instance, I'm a good twenty years older than the girl sitting next to Thomas. What would formerly have been a "legitimate interest" has become, simply because of the passage of time, "criminal paedophilia." A quantitative change has become a qualitative one. No doubt about it, she's underage. Sixteen or seventeen. Eighteen at the very most. She's right next to the door—and poised on the edge of her chair, as though she were about to take flight—as shy and wild as a gazelle. Her eyes keep darting here and there as though they didn't know what to settle on. Will they meet mine? She's really very charming. The way her hands keep smoothing her skirt over her skinny, nervous thighs. The face framed by a shock of hair—almost a helmet, whereas her features are so delicate. The nose a bit pointed, maybe the collar-bone too. What about the ilium?

There's something quite fascinating about her. Too bad. If I so much as spoke to her, Hélène would make some sarcastic remark about my future as a dirty old man. Everyone's in favour of sexual liberation, provided the age groups remain airtight. And of course it's inconceivable that a seventeen-year-old girl could be found interesting for reasons other than sexual; that she might have her own ideas, her own opinions, her own problems, and want to talk them over with someone. I'd be the male aggressor right away. Probably in her eyes as well, for that matter. She must be constantly harassed in the street. With a body like that, and such a forlorn look on her face, it's more than likely. I wonder what she's doing here... Thomas will have noted a lot more details; he'll share them with me afterwards. For someone who doesn't like women, he's remarkably observant on that score. He'll be able to confirm my guess about the ilium, at least.

VARIATIO VII: INFINITE

Hélène

Even the chairs are special. I'm sure they bought them at the flea market for next to nothing, and Bernald Thorer himself must have stripped and varnished them; apparently he's been doing a lot of handiwork since he stopped writing. And he's the one who painted the flowers on the inside panel of the harpsichord, after a 17th-century Flemish design. Those microscopic petals are so beautiful... I get impatient just looking at them. Like when I'm at the Decorative Arts Museum...I go from one room to another, looking at all those miniature objects, each of which took months or even years of effort—goldwork, woodwork, ironwork, all that concentration, all that energy... It depresses me, I don't know why. Perhaps because I just can't see the point—and yet it's beautiful, I can't deny that. Beauty is something finished. I never finish anything. As if that would imply "finishing it off"—killing it. Or maybe it's just that I can't. So I tend to purchase things that are new, ready-made—sometimes they're beautiful, too, but it's not the same. I'd much rather live in a house like this one, I know it would be better suited to my temperament—but I'm afraid I wouldn't be able to make the effort. The same with cooking—I love real home-made dishes but I'm afraid I won't be able to follow the recipes, so I always end up making the same things, things that don't require any preparation. I'd never be able to grow herbs in flowerpots, for instance. I'd be too miserable if they died and I was responsible. Or if they didn't grow at all—I'd take it as a sign. Pierre says he couldn't care less, he'd just as soon eat out, and we can afford restaurants now that he makes more money than before, but still I can't help wishing we had a real home. I never feel we're actually building something together, it always just stays the same, we live from day to day in the pleasure of the moment. And it's true there's a lot of pleasure… but it makes me anxious not to know where we're heading. I have this need for security—maybe it's because of my middle-class background, but that's the way I feel.

At work, it's just the opposite; it's the security that makes me anxious. I'm terrified of turning into a dippy old lady. Teaching the same high school French course year after year… I know it's something I do well, the students think I'm okay, sometimes I even manage to inspire them with a love for literature, and it isn't totally numbing like factory work… But when I look at the people around me who've been teaching twenty or thirty years and are counting the time they have to "put in" before retirement, it makes my blood run cold. I can see myself becoming exactly like them… I'm already good at playing their game, complaining about all the papers I have to mark and how in winter I have to catch the train when it's still dark outside… I can just see my concerns getting narrower and narrower, and me winding up a crotchety old lady like Madame Bonnaud. But every time I broach the subject with Pierre, he tells me to take up some new interest—you've got lots of time, you only have two days a week of classes, you're free to do whatever you like. And I don't dare tell him the truth, which is that I have no idea what I like. Every time I pick up a book, I wonder if I've made the right choice. In order to read So-and-so, you must first have read What's-his-name…and after a while all I can see are the gaps in my knowledge and I feel like banging my head against the wall. Even being a French teacher makes me feel like an impostor: when I was in high school I thought teachers knew everything. I feel I know nothing—not even where to start. People who know what they want out of life have always amazed me. How are you supposed to choose your future profession at the age of fourteen or fifteen? Everyone else seemed to find it natural; they wrote exams and ended up, as if by magic, following the paths cut out for them. As for me…my grades were good and studying came easily; since I was a girl I got sent into Literature, and I said okay, fine, and things just went on that way until I found myself with a teaching job. I feel as if I'd never made a real choice in my life.

How does it happen I'm the only one who recognizes the holes in her intelligence? Other people, be they idiots or geniuses, always seem convinced of what they do and say. The minute a sentence is out of my mouth—even if no one contradicts it—my conviction deserts me. Yet there are any number of blockheads who spout inanities and look utterly self-satisfied… Everyone is self-satisfied. I'm the only one who doesn't draw satisfaction from herself, the only one with holes in her head. No matter how many books I read—during vacations I gobble down two a day—it doesn't help. The holes are still there, black and gaping. When I listen to a conversation between Pierre and his friends, I really admire them. Not only do they know what they think, they express themselves so extraordinarily well, using allusions, comparisons, humour, indignation, sometimes hilarious pantomime… They really go all the way; they know how to commit themselves.

And yet I know Pierre respects my intelligence. Once I asked him whether his head ever felt empty, and he said, "Frankly, no." He doesn't seem to be aware of the asymmetry between us—the fact that he has passions and I don't. Sometimes I think it's all for the better—if he knew how much I depend on him to guide me intellectually, he'd probably drop me; he can't stand the idea of playing a fatherly role. He's extremely sensitive on that point. He hates being teased about his penchant for younger women. First it was Liliane and then me… I'm four years younger than Liliane. He says her beauty has faded somewhat now. It doesn't even occur to him that it might scare me to hear that… It seems awfully unfair to care less about someone just because time has altered her body. Liliane's personality may have grown richer, more complex, more human than when he lived with her—I don't know, she and I hardly ever talk on the phone anymore—but that doesn't interest him; the only thing that interests him is that "her beauty has faded somewhat." He assures me that I'm as lovely as ever, that I get younger every day… The thing is, I wish I didn't have to get younger. I wish I could age with a sense of tranquillity, with the feeling I was loved. That's how I imagine Liliane's life with Bernald Thorer: ageing with tranquillity. Maybe Pierre just says that about Liliane to make me feel better. He knows I've always been afraid I was nothing but a replacement for her. He swears it isn't true—that their relationship had fallen to pieces and they were filled with mutual resentment—but I've never been able to rid myself of that suspicion. It haunts me even now. After all, when we met, I was just another "conquest" as far as they were concerned. Maybe that wasn't the word they would have used, but that's what it amounted to. A younger girl, a nymphet they could cajole and seduce. And they were so seductive it made my head spin—they reminded me of the Fitzgeralds.

So at the end of a dinner party at their place, where there'd been an excess of people and alcohol, the crowd started thinning out and finally just the three of us were left… The white sheepskin rug we stretched out on to listen to music is here in the front hall; it must have been Liliane's… Pierre put on a record, harpsichord music by Scarlatti, then he lay down and put an arm around each of us and turned towards me and brushed my lips with his. I was a bit confused, I'd never been in a situation like that before, but everything was so gentle, and Liliane was smiling… She started stroking the hair at the nape of my neck. And it's true that I wanted Pierre very badly. He was so fine, so attentive, so cultivated... and I just let go. We undressed each other very slowly, we'd stopped talking but the music went on playing, Liliane kissed me passionately on the mouth and I felt the overwhelming smoothness of a woman's skin for the first time. I was trembling with emotion; now it was Liliane I wanted, without quite knowing what that might mean... Then the floating feeling ceased; the record had come to an end but we'd gone too far to stop and turn it over. I was just a little bit too wide awake. I kept wondering how the three of us would actually go about making love together. I saw that Pierre was very aroused and suddenly I had the unpleasant feeling of being part of a *tableau vivant*—wasn't he aroused by the *image* of two beautiful, naked young women at his side—and wouldn't the tenderness between Liliane and myself be subsumed by that image? Suddenly the whole thing seemed contrived, though I couldn't have said exactly why. Then I felt ashamed. I told myself that this resistance was due to my Puritan upbringing. I rebuked myself for not being able to love these very loving people... In the end, Pierre entered me, with Liliane caressing both our chests at once, and I didn't feel a thing. I kept seeing the whole scene from the outside—like a troop of acrobats or an erotic engraving—and it left me totally cold. Luckily he came almost immediately and the three of us fell asleep, lying there on the rug just as we were—too drunk to go to bed. The next morning Liliane and I talked it over. Pierre had already left for work. We made some coffee and went to drink it in the untouched bed. She told me that she, too, had felt a bit ill at ease—she could never quite grasp all the emotions that went through her at times like that; it was hard to tell the difference between sincerity and wilfullness; of course, to see another woman being penetrated by the man she loved didn't leave her indifferent, but after all, jealousy was a social construct and she wanted to overcome it—and, finally, she really did like me very much. We kissed lingeringly but we didn't make love.

Since Pierre and I have been living together, he's never suggested we do something of that kind… I told him it had made me nervous and I think he understood. On the other hand, it's quite possible he's been unfaithful to me…but the very idea of that is sheer torture so in any case I'd rather—

VARIATIO VIII: JACK-SCREW

Carpenter

…the only one who didn't live in an Ivory Tower. The time he paid my way to accompany him to the States, the Deep South, I could see he was interested in everything. Just like a kid. Wanted to know all about the people we met, the towns we went through, everything. Once we lost our way and drove down this guy's dirt road. He started waving a hunting rifle at us, yelling "You bastards!"—and as we backed up to turn around Bernald said, "How does it happen that the word bastard is an insult in English and not in French?"—meanwhile I was peeing my pants. Violence fascinated him. Not in any morbid sense; it just preoccupied him. Two of his books were on the subject. Another time, we were walking around this Black neighbourhood, the only Whites in the street, and the guys sitting on their front steps were giving us really evil looks. "It does you good to be the other for once," Bernald said, "if only to get some idea of what the Arabs have to deal with back at home." He was right, too—I suddenly felt like it was weird to have white skin, like it wasn't normal. I kept saying to myself, "Boy, those Blacks wouldn't dare look at us that way if they knew this guy with the stooped shoulders was one of the biggest brains in the whole wide world." But it's true we were on their territory, gawking at them like a couple of dumb tourists.

Bernald got involved in the Algerian War, too—and not just to sign petitions or lend his name to the cause. All those years we saw a lot of each other. We used to talk about politics and he'd always have some original point of view. In '68 he was the only one in all of Paris who managed to stay lucid. Understood what was going on but kept his distance. Said he didn't like the word revolution, to begin with. Didn't like cops or state troopers or soldiers; didn't like loudmouth leftist leaders either. Didn't like leaders or heroes in general—"people who yell WE so loud they drown out all the I's," I remember him saying once. He meant it, too—he practised what he preached. For example he didn't get off on quarrels in the papers. He just didn't get off on war, even when the weapons were just words.

I wasn't used to being around people like that. I'd see his picture in bookstore windows and I'd think, it can't be for real; somebody that famous can't possibly be interested in me—I know my old man never had friends like that. But it was for real, he was interested in me, he'd never say he was busy if I rang him up in the middle of the day, like I used to sometimes when I had problems. For example when Suzanne flew the coop or when I lost my job. He'd say, Come on, let's have a drink together. Do you feel like stopping by? He was living alone at the time and I'd go over to his place. There were books everywhere, on the floor, in the kitchen… That's where we used to drink, in the kitchen, and he'd tell me his problems, too, how his mind was a blank that day, or how he wondered if writing was still worth it, I remember once he was feeling low and asked me if maybe he could become a carpenter like me. I said carpentry wasn't something you could learn overnight, it took time. I'd done seven years apprenticeship myself but I'd be glad to show him a few basics. So we got together once a week for about a year. Every Saturday afternoon I'd come over and he'd put on some music—really good stuff, too, jazz records from the thirties—and we'd have a beer or two while we were working. I showed him about tools and materials, how to tell good wood when you see it, the whole bit. He paid attention and really threw himself into it. I must say I was surprised. He wasn't kidding, he took it seriously and learned a lot. I think it did us both a lot of good to be seeing each other regularly and doing something together.

Later on, when I moved out to the suburbs, we lost touch for a while. Things were looking up for me—I'd found a job I liked, but it was pretty exhausting and I didn't feel like coming back into town in the evening. Bernald would call me every now and then to see how I was. I thought things must be looking up for him, too, but maybe I was wrong. If he'd been in good shape, he wouldn't have fallen into the clutches of the witch. No, honestly—I just don't understand what he sees in that woman. I could practically kill her—and not just because she took my buddy away from me. She's not on the up-and-up, that's all. There's something shady about her. She reminds me of that song Bernald used to play sometimes, he translated the words for me once, "Sad-Eyed Lady of the Lowlands." She plays the sad-eyed lady, that's what she does. She looks right at you with her big, lost-little-girl eyes, and you start to squirm. Why does she look at you that way? As if she wanted you to tell her something—but what? So you rack your brains…and meanwhile, still with that feeble feminine look on her face, she robs you of your soul. She's really like those witches that used to steal people's souls. She didn't get mine—I can't talk to her, anyhow; I have nothing to say to her. She's not like Bernald—he can talk to anybody. She just looks at you without a word—she uses silence like it was talking… Anyhow, she's stolen his soul, that's for sure. I hate to see the way he is now, so soft, so completely under her control. Yes, Dear. Whatever you say, Dear. And since they've been together I haven't been able to talk to him either. When I come here, it's not the same as his place when he lived alone. It's no fun anymore, I don't know. He talks about what's going on, and I just can't understand why he stopped writing. Not that I used to read his books—but that was his way of keeping up the struggle. It's just not enough to struggle over two for tea and tea for two—I'll never get used to it.

The sad-eyed lady looks a bit pale and drawn tonight. Maybe what she needs is a good slap in the face. Wake her up. Put a little colour in her cheeks. Why's she always dressed in black, huh? Never seen her wear any other colour. Like everybody she ever loved was dead. Except she doesn't love anybody. She's the one who's dead. A ghost. You can't touch her. She's right next to you but she isn't there. You don't know where the hell she is. In another world. She smiles at you, you feel like socking her in the mouth. Not too hard—just enough to cut her lip. Just to see if she's really made of flesh and blood. She doesn't look human. What's she got underneath that dress? Has she got breasts like a real woman? No breasts. No hips. No ass. Skinny as an eel. Slips between your fingers. What's she got on under all that black? She doesn't even wear a bra. Does she wear panties? Black ones? Black lace panties she bought in a fancy store? Or in a foreign country? She's the one Bernald takes with him now when he travels. What's she got on underneath? What does she look like? She can't have a pussy like ordinary women. Her black dress is like a second skin sticking to her skin, you feel like tearing it off. You feel like tearing off those panties. You feel like grabbing her by the shoulders and shaking her—are you going to stop this bullshit? You bitch! Stop acting like a ghost! Have you got a pussy like everybody else? It must be cold. It must be cold and dry as a tomb. Does it even have a hole in it? Huh, you bitch? You feel like grabbing her by the hair and jerking her head from side to side. You feel like crushing her jaw with one hand. She wouldn't even yell. She wouldn't even cry. She hasn't got any tears. She's dry and cold, Lady Untouchable. She'd just keep staring at you with those eyes of hers—why are you doing this? What have I done to you? A look of reproach on her face—"Oh, how I've suffered in life! Look how sad I am! Look how dead I am!"—fucking bitch.

It's no use. You'd let go of her. Drop her. Let her die, if

that's what she wants. It's her business. They can both go to hell, for all I care. So can everyone in this room, and they can take their lousy music with them. This isn't what Bernald used to listen to, this tinkle-tinkle in a chamber pot. Just wait till it's over, then high-tail it out of here. Never set foot in this fucking house again. Marie told me I shouldn't come here anymore. She was right. I would have been better off in front of the TV set. They're not like us, she said. I explained about Bernald, how he used to be different. But she doesn't like intellectuals, that's all there is to it. As far as she's concerned they're a bunch of lazybones who don't know what it means to work. She's right, in a way. When you look at the jewellery the witch is wearing… and everybody else's fancy clothes… They're a bunch of parasites, when you come right down to it. I worked ten hours before coming here today. Same thing tomorrow. It's okay for them to go to bed at midnight, they can sleep in any day of the week. Just answer the phone for us, will you, Mademoiselle? I saw the maid when I came in. She doesn't have the right to listen to the music—naturally. There weren't enough chairs? Maybe that's why. So sorry, my dear, but you can come back afterwards and empty the ashtrays. I know what I'm talking about—my mother was a cleaning-lady. When she was the witch's age, she was already an old woman. Besides which she was fat, and the fatter she got the less she could work. You've got to have money to be as skinny as the witch. Madame eats nothing but caviar and smoked salmon, you understand. Doesn't even know what noodles and potatoes look like. Never had them on her plate.

I had nothing else when I was growing up. First time Marie made me boiled potatoes, I threw the plate in her face. She caught on right away. I earn a decent wage now—no more boiled potatoes for me. We're not living in poverty like my mom and dad. I bring home enough money so she doesn't have to work; the least she can do is put some effort into the cooking. She caught on, though, said she was sorry. It's never happened again.

VARIATIO IX: FILIATION

Madame Fournier

I won't do the same thing to Nathalie. Maybe she thinks that's what she wants, but I'll put my foot down. Last Friday, all the parents were invited to the school audition, and she sang—but only in the chorus. "I want to take voice lessons, I want to join the Opera"—and I say no; I tell her she's deluding herself. That whole world sets her dreaming. It seems so brilliant to her, but it's rotten to the core. The competition. The aggressiveness. I don't want her to have to deal with that. She'll thank me someday. I had to learn the hard way. She should benefit from my experience. I refuse to put her through the torture my mother put me through. I was only three years old, we were taking a nap together, and she said: "One day you'll be a pianist, darling. You'll wear a long white dress and when you come on stage everyone will applaud. You'll sit down at the piano and play beautiful music—Brahms, Beethoven—and after every piece the clapping will get louder. They'll call you back for an encore—then another, and another—and when it's over they'll bring you roses. You'll travel all over the world, be greeted everywhere with open arms. Yes, darling. Provided you work hard."

The school audition brought back unbelievably painful memories. I hadn't thought about that time for ages—the sheer madness of it. An auditorium containing over a hundred children between the ages of seven and nine, most of them accompanied by their mothers. My own mother couldn't come that day; I was alone. One after the other, in alphabetical order, the children were called up to play a Mozart *adagio* in front of a jury of ten adults. Each of them would receive a score out of a hundred. The results would be made known only after everyone had played. It went on and on and on. The atmosphere was thick and dusty, the clock hands seemed to have stopped moving. My name being close to the end of the alphabet, I thought my turn would never come. I wished the whole thing were already over or that it had never begun.

You have to play the piece by heart. I must have played it a thousand times. It's there, somewhere in my fingers. I hear it being played, over and over and over, and I seem to recognize it less and less. I start to sweat. My forehead and my hands grow moist. What if my fingers slip off the keyboard? What if I fall off the stool? I'll never be able to climb the steps to the stage in the first place. I watch the others to see how they do it. I don't know any of them. They're not my friends. No one has sat down in the same row as me. The auditorium is gigantic. After each execution of the adagio, the applause is feeble and lukewarm. My heart beats and that's all I can hear. Its thumping fills me from head to toe. My hands are damp, exuding sweat. I'm afraid I'm going to wet my pants. I'm afraid I'm going to dissolve—melt into a puddle on the floor.

I wipe my hands on my white dress and leave a streak. It's a new dress; my mother will be mad. No, I'll never go home again—when this is over, I'll run down to the river and drown myself. Then she'll realize how much she loved me—when I'm dead.

I hear my name being called. My turn has come. So time hadn't stopped after all. I stand and begin to glide towards the stage as in a dream. Suddenly I find myself next to the grand piano. In fact I'm already seated on the stool. The keyboard stretches out in front of me like an endless, black and white beach. Never have I seen anything like it in my life. I lift my hands: they, too, are unrecognizable. I have no idea how to go about using them. I'm mesmerized by the juxtaposition of all these unlikely objects: stool, keyboard, hands. Finally, the latter start to move of their own accord. The keys seem to resist. My wrists are made of jelly. I play the piece almost at random; more than half the notes are inaudible. The end is approaching. All I need to do is play the final chord, and then I can drown myself. My hands are suspended above the keyboard. They drop. No, that's not it. They came down in the wrong place. There, that's it. The applause breaks out—louder than for the others. I return to my seat.

When it's all over, my score is more than honourable—not tops, of course, I don't win any prizes—but still, I'm in the "excellent" category. My mother will be proud of me.

It took me a long time to understand that applause, but now it's obvious to me— the adults wanted to see the children suffer, and I had suffered excellently. I had embodied their sense of powerlessness, their fear of failure. I was "excellent" because I'd come within a hair's breadth of breaking down, and yet I hadn't broken down. Not then, anyway. I went on like that for ten more years. With an interruption at the age of thirteen (puberty makes children capricious), when I decided to stop classical piano and start jazz. My mother reacted as though the world had fallen apart. "After all the money I've spent so you could have the best teacher in Geneva? No, young lady, as long as you're still living under my roof, you may not do whatever takes your fancy." So— until I was seventeen. And then my world fell apart.

"Why don't you try giving your first concerts in old-folks' homes around the city? It won't pay, but it will get you used to playing in front of people. As it is, you freeze up if someone walks into the room while you're practising. They'll be an indulgent audience—and you'll be bringing a bit of sunshine into their lives."

First concert. Pale green halls with doors ajar, monsters behind every one of them. Men and women, alone, dying of loneliness, huddled in bed like so many mouldy warts. By the time I get to the main room, I'm already tense and apprehensive. A dozen old ladies are lying in wait for me. They point to the piano—it's a Robert Stather; I'm familiar with its nasal tonality. What am I doing here? Ever submissive, I cross the room and sit down. It will be Chopin's *Valse Brillante*. I start off just a shade too fast. That doesn't matter. I'll show them. I make it through the difficult passages, trying to keep in mind that this is something *beautiful*; that all of us are here to share *the most sublime thing in the world*—music. What was Chopin thinking about when he wrote this waltz? Definitely not about the misery he was preparing for all the pianists of the future. Perhaps he was in Majorca with George Sand, trembling with cold and fever in their unheated monastery; perhaps he wrote the *Brillante* so as to transport them into another, magical world… Suddenly, in the midst of a *pianissimo*, one of the old ladies utters distinctly, "My niece plays this piece better than that!"

I stopped abruptly, left the room, and never gave another concert in my life. Because that's the true meaning of concerts nowadays, Nathalie. Classical music has been totally perverted; it only reflects the neuroses of our society. When you tune in to "The Critics' Tribunal" on Sunday afternoons, do you ever think about what those words mean? A *tribunal*? Of *critics*? A bunch of judges who give free rein to their sadistic impulses, praising one musician the better to condemn another? Can't you hear the way they speak? "Oh, yes, Philip II's aria in *Don Carlo* as sung by Boris Christoff—it brings tears to my eyes, it's utterly divine!" "Yes, yes, very moving indeed, without a shadow of a doubt." "And now, let's hear another excerpt, considerably gayer than the preceding one…"

No one hears anything. Neither the despotic parents, nor the martyred children, nor the critics' tribunal, nor the people in this room. What they enjoy playing is not music, but the monstrous game of being music lovers—whereas their true love is the suffering of musicians.

I thought jazz might save me—at least it was alive and

free—outlaw music. Unfortunately, for me it was too late. For the rest of my life, every time I sit down at the piano I'll be wearing a long white dress. I'd gladly give my right arm to be able to improvise like Keith Jarrett. But it just doesn't happen, and it never will. What I have in my fingers are the trills, the slides and the *appoggiatura* of my childhood; I'll never be able to get rid of them. More than anything in the world, I wish that when people came over, I could make them vibrate to unearthly strains—syncopated rhythms, harmonies in mauve and green… but I know what would come out: the classical pieces I've been playing by heart since I was seventeen—and with mistakes, to boot. Flagrant inaccuracies. It just isn't worth it.

You do have a lovely voice, Nathalie. I love listening when you sing at home from time to time. But you simply mustn't turn music into a career. Believe me, you'd only make yourself miserable. You'd be forced to prostitute your voice, to compare it with other voices, to sacrifice your love for music in order to succeed. That's the way it is. It's far better to go on singing like a bird than put your vocal chords through all kinds of strenuous and boring exercises. All I want to do is spare you the torture I went through. If you start listening to your voice to see if it's better than someone else's, you'll stop hearing its melody. It happens to rock singers, too—please believe me, it's a ruthless world. Every single one of them needs drugs just to keep going. People are so eager to watch them suffer. People don't know what to do with their own death wish, so they pay a hundred dollars to see Janis Joplin or Bette Midler slowly committing suicide. Is tonight the night she'll fall to pieces—right there on the stage? Will The Voice go slack and slither down into a moan? Nathalie darling, I'm telling the truth. I've been through it and it's left me atrophied; I so much want you to be whole and happy—

VARIATIO X: LOSS

Writer

...the editorial board would get together every morning at ten for a brainstorming session. Sylvère would start out with some piece of national or international news, and the discussion would bubble and boil. Our enthusiasm knew no limits—neither did our disingenuousness. The list of employees grew longer every day. Sylvère hired everyone that walked in the door—the friend of a friend, the unemployed shorthand typist who wanted to be recycled as a typesetter for *The Other Day*... We were crazy about this project, and we shot for the moon. Even before the first issue came out, we'd opened a cafeteria for the employees and a day-care centre for their children. Most nights we'd hang around the office until two in the morning, reading the dispatches and drinking beer. When Sylvère allotted each of us an office, it was like a big family moving into a new house: this will be your room, this one will be mine... We were so thrilled with the intercom that we couldn't stop calling each other up to make sure it worked. Then it came time to paint the offices, and for three days we lived in total hilarity, all of us dressed up in white overalls, messing around like kids in a sandbox. Lili was especially childlike—it was the only time I ever saw her that way, with a sort of clarity in her face—she'd run around from one office to another, wearing a white painter's cap and exclaiming joyfully—"What a beautiful poster!" "How did you get that shade of apricot?" Even Sylvère, who was dying to get the newspaper on its feet, didn't do anything to cut our antics short.

I haven't thought about those days for ages. "Those days" is accurate, in fact; the whole thing was over in a matter of days. Looking back, it seems like little more that a hiccup after the big feast of '68. We thought we could prove the ability of the Left to be intelligent, lucid, amusing and diversified—I don't remember what other adjectives we used in the editorial of the first issue. Sylvère relieved himself of several hundred thousand francs in the space of a few months, and *The Other Day* bit the dust within two weeks of its launching. When he realized bankruptcy was imminent, Sylvère called a meeting and explained to all of us that we couldn't go on under present conditions, but that we'd resume publication after taking the time to think things over. We went out and had dinner in Les Halles—all fifty of us were his guests—a sort of funeral service. The melancholic gaiety around that table… I'm surprised at how nostalgic it makes me. I can remember the exact taste of the Sancerre, the mountains of oysters, the hubbub of our voices… Summer camp was over and we were going to have to go our separate ways. The dream of an ideal community of minds had evaporated in the brutal glare of Giscardian realism. When we woke up, we found ourselves alone again and had to carry on as best we could. Some of the women started to work for feminist papers, resigning themselves to a few more years of unpaid militancy. Jacques got himself a column as musical critic for *The Day*—thanks to Sylvère, of course, who immediately took refuge in his daddy's paper. Lili, who would have been in charge of the "Culture" section, crawled back into the harpsichord-shell she'd abandoned since adolescence... Others wound up on the couch. I returned to my words, with a taste of death in my mouth.

We've grown older. Not dramatically so—this hardly matches the final scene of *Remembrance of Things Past*—but there's no doubt about it, we're getting on. It's touching to see that Lili now has a few white hairs among the black. Sylvère is ageing well: he'll be able to play the dynamic young editor-in-chief for years to come. Jacques is starting to go to pot, though; that I didn't expect. I wonder if he's still in love with Lili. It was really something, the way they tore each other apart. Once I advised Lili to leave him. She'd come over to my place in the afternoon to make love. "What the hell is this sexual freedom you allow each other? How can you believe you're still in love, when both of you fall for everything that moves?" "I don't know, I don't know"—her face in the pillow—"I can't remember. It has something to do with Charles Fourier. There's the pivotal relationship, and then there are the butterflies flitting around it. Apparently the best way of preserving a couple." She was laughing in a very unfunny way. "Shit," I said. "Move in with me." "Are you crazy? How could I live with someone who beats me?" "What are you talking about? I don't beat you." "Yes, you do. Every time we make love, you hit me on the ass—it hurts." "Really? I don't do it on purpose. Do you want to hit me now, to get even?" "No. I want you to tell me the story of the three old princesses who fell in love with the young man." "All right. But only if you promise not to fall asleep until I've gotten one sentence farther than last time. Do you remember where we were?" "Yes… The one who retrieved her youth had just explained to her sisters that all they had to do was go get their faces planed." She burst out laughing, just like a little girl. "That's right. Now, close your eyes and I'll start all over again. Once upon a time, there were three old princesses…" This story did put her to sleep, as if by enchantment, every time I told it. She never got enough sleep. She was afraid of time going by without her. When she awoke, she'd scrutinize her face in the mirror as the violet light of dusk infused the room— "As long as it's rings and not pouches, I don't mind."

Incredible how well I remember. Only music gives me leave to do this… in the sense of military "leave." Like Lili, I'm constantly struggling with time—sucked into it. Perhaps that's less true for her since she's been living with Bernald Thorer. We haven't talked about it. For me it only gets worse and worse—this feeling that if I don't fill up every minute of the day, I could end up doing nothing. I could go sit on a park bench like a bum and watch the sun cross the sky from east to west, watch the mothers go by with their little ones, the little ones get bigger, the girls turn into young ladies and then into mothers themselves… it's terrifying. So I lock myself in, make sure I have everything I need—unlined hardcover notebooks, fine-point felt pens, coffee, cigarettes—and then the race against the clock begins. Anxiety seizes me by the throat and makes me gasp for breath, but also makes me write. That's the only thing that counts—and it's unbelievable the way I treat it like a job. If I had to punch in at a factory, I couldn't be more fanatical about counting the time I put in. Whenever the phone rings, I look at my watch before answering—it's absurd. When a dinner party goes on past midnight, I start worrying about how I'm going to get up the next morning, as though I had a boss. Objectively, of course, I have all the time in the world. No one's threatening me with a deadline. As a matter of fact, people love the image of the artist struggling endlessly with his creation. But if I don't devote a certain number of hours a day to writing, I cut my own privileges—for example, I refuse myself permission to go to the movies. Like a Catholic who doesn't have the right to take Communion without Confession. Because if one day were to go by without my writing, there'd be no reason for the other days not to follow suit. If my vigilance were to slacken, time might accelerate while my back was turned—it might advance by leaps and bounds, and whole years would vanish into the trap-door of my momentary distraction.

There are two exceptions to this infernal logic, and only two: love and music. For them, and only for them, can I bear wasting time—because they occur outside of language. Both attempt to "say something," yet both come to full flower in the attempt, the intention to speak; they have to do with language, yet are simultaneously beneath and beyond it. (Lili says they're untranslatable, which is the same thing.) And the reason they bestow on me the exceptional privilege of living in the present is that, in spite of everything, they're circumscribed in time. You can't go on fucking indefinitely; every piece of music has a beginning and an end. I'm safe because I know in advance that the disappearance of language is only temporary.

This is not a waste of precious time, but rather a precious waste of time.

All the same, I myself could never have been a musician. Lili and I have often talked about this: how creative is some-one who only interprets another person's creation? She says that without actors, plays wouldn't be theatre; that classical music would be lifeless paper were it not for instrumentalists. She's right, of course—and I can imagine how marvellous it must be to bring to life the potential beauty sealed up in silent scores. But it would be unthinkable for me—too demanding, and at the same time not demanding enough. I could never accept the rigours of performance—I'm too unstable. I couldn't stand having to be in full possession of my powers, in front of other people, at a given moment—this is also why I've never enjoyed teaching. I could never get used to the idea that my performance was being judged *in time*, and compared with someone else's. Writing can't be judged that way, on the basis of objective criteria. This, of course, doesn't prevent the critics from proffering their inanities. A recent article in *The Day* said that my latest book was halfway between the avant-garde and nostalgic classicism. In other words I'm running on the spot, like a guinea-pig in its cage. But at least that imbecile didn't have the right to be with me in my study, looking over my shoulder as I worked... My highest hope for my books is that people who love each other will want to read them out loud. Like fairy tales in the olden days. Families gathered around fireplaces, lovers in bed; that would be truly wonderful...

VARIATIO XI: ACID

Christine

…but the charm is dead. This house used to be one of my Places, one of my havens. It isn't anymore. Lili, how can you betray me like this? I thought you understood. We talked about it so often—don't you remember? Now everyone's betrayed me. You used to listen, nod your head and say—me too, I'm frightened too, yes, the way people live is grotesque, I know what you mean about the absurdity of it all… No one else has ever made me feel the way you did—not only understanding everything I said but giving me the courage to express it, the courage to believe it wasn't just baby whinings but adult agony. I told you I even felt betrayed by the philosophers of the absurd—Kierkegaard, Sartre, Laing—I resented them for having been to the bottom of this horror— our horror, meaninglessness—and then having calmly returned to the surface, like when you push off from the floor of a swimming pool, only to write about it and publish it and use it to become famous. And now even you have betrayed me, Lili, even you are playing at *épater les bourgeois*. Are these your friends nowadays—the burjoys? I used to like the word burjoys—before I learned to speak French—my brother and

I used to get a kick out of pronouncing the most sophisticated French words with the most dreadful English accent: "You're looking awfully svelt and deboner today, ma chair." When I lived in Paris, I stopped using the English r and I missed it; sometimes I'd walk home going rrr-rrr just to make sure I could still pronounce it; I told you about this and you said I should cultivate my American accent, it sounded very chic—I was amazed that English could sound chic to anyone's ears. For me it's vulgar, my mother tongue, my mother's tongue and her thick lips, her tongue that twisted and turned and lashed out at me, my mother's mouth, red lipstick that leaves spots, white teeth, strands of saliva between the upper and lower lips, how to tear the English language apart, tear my tongue to shreds, but the words will always fall right-side up like a cat and people will always keep on going, chin-up, chin-chin, if it's not valid keep on going anyway, find out what you have in common, homonym, *comment, commère, comme mère, mare, cauchemar, mare au diable, diabolo menthe, mentir, m'en tirer, m'étirer, métier,* whatever they do they're sure they're right to be doing it, the factory workers, the craftsmen, the businessmen, the chiefs of State, the intellectuals, I'll never be like them, I prefer to undermine. Lili, do you remember how we used to say that people who were *convaincus,* convinced, were always *vaincus,* vanquished— because they'd had to overpower and strangle all their doubts? They were *cons vaincus,* vanquished assholes—far worse than those who killed themselves. Remember?

How many floors? That's the only thing I felt like asking

when your friend threw herself out the window. How many floors are needed to accomplish death? To stop the ticking of the heart-clock that drives us mad? I remember your telling me about her internment in the mental hospital (the loony-bin, as we say in my country): her regression, her dazed appearance, and the alarming metamorphosis of her body. She grew fatter by the day, as if to build a screen of flesh between herself and the world (but now that flesh would quickly melt, and be definitively replaced by the bone structure). All she did was go through the successive stages of despair more rapidly than you or I, assisted in her progress by the psychiatrists, the physicians and her mother; confronted with her failure and forced to rub her nose in it. You, Lili, could see her death approaching and settling in, slowly but surely. In the end she ran to meet it (hers was not a political suicide; the newspapers didn't mention it the next day). Wasn't she right, though? Not to want to watch the pain she was inflicting on others anymore, or bear the pain she herself was undergoing? Why do we stubbornly go on reasoning like mountain-climbers—"I live my life *because it's there*"—exactly as though life were a mountain that could be "successfully" or "unsuccessfully" climbed, with foothills and a summit? How high does one have to climb before one has the right to give up? How many floors?

You won't kill yourself now, Lili—that much is clear. You're leaving me alone. You're settling down into life. You're letting time go by. Don't you remember our acid trip? How can you give a concert once you've lived through that? I don't understand. You and I experienced, together, the infinite expansion of each second. We shared a cheese sandwich, and each mouthful was a fresh burst of ecstasy. *This* is what people gulp down without thinking, their elbows propped on a lunch-counter, between two appointments? We drank red wine and called it nectar *des déesses*. Your cushions were magnificent to our eyes; we spent an eternity exclaiming over the beauty of their patterns. Touching each other's bodies was a miracle. You put Bach's *Magnificat* on the stereo and every note resounded with awful meaning, shaking us to the bowels. We clutched at each other, your fingers explored every feature of my face, and you said: I wish I could play your body like an organ, I want to know all of your stops, *tous tes jeux*, and I heard: *tous tes je*, all of your selves. I put my head between your knees and looked up at you, you were beautiful, you were horrendous, you were monumental, I caressed your clitoris with my tongue, you were dying, I thought we wouldn't be able to bear the intensity of what we were feeling—life, we were alive, it was too, too powerful, we were bodies at long last, bodies with organs, saliva, chiz, the salt smell of it in your vagina, you were trembling from head to foot, even your arms trembled as they stroked my back, your thin and fragile arms inhabited by that thin and fragile entity known as life. *Est-ce possible que tu aies oublié cela?*

Every day I struggle not to forget it. I go to work in offices, I look at the people around me and I wonder—do they so much as know they are alive? I'm scared even to read the newspaper headlines: men will still be killing and killing and killing each other—by the thousand, by the million—just as they always have, for nothing. Sometimes I just can't bear it anymore. Last winter there was a day that was worse than most—there are days when all it takes is for a waiter to make a snide remark and I burst into tears—I called up Dominique at eleven o'clock at night. I said, "There's a plane for Montreal at midnight. Meet me at the airport. Bring your guitar. I've got some acid." "But don't you have to go to work tomorrow morning?" "Yes, but not till nine o'clock. I can catch the seven-thirty flight back." And so, sitting on a bench in Mount Royal Park, we sucked the tiny bits of blotter stained with pink and watched the giant city at our feet turn gradually into a fairyland. The lights began to dance beneath our eyes, seeming to spell out words, fantastic symbols it was our duty to decipher. Dominique began to play a Canadian Indian song I've always loved:

Oh, the moon shines bright on pretty Red Wing
The night winds sighing
The night birds crying
And far, far away her love lies sleeping
While Red Wing's weeping
Her heart away.

The moon was orange-hued and we were starting to notice the cold. There was snow on the ground—old, dirty snow—but we didn't feel like being in an apartment. Around four in the morning, we decided to walk a bit; we were afraid of not being able to judge how cold it was, and joked about how we might be discovered on the bench the next morning, an ice sculpture entitled "The Death of Music." A little way down the path we came upon an old man—not exactly a bum, but, well, someone who was spending the night in a park with a bottle of cheap red wine. We started talking to him and it was love at first sight. It turned out he was an Indian. He asked me to play something on my flute. I hadn't even taken it out yet. When I removed it from its case, it looked, quite literally, like a magic flute—I felt as if, once I'd assembled the three pieces, it would be an omnipotent magic wand. It was glowing as though lit up from within, its metal coming directly from Aladdin's cave. Shakily I brought it to my mouth, scarcely believing I had the right to make it sing. The air was so cold that my wet lips instantly stuck to the mouthpiece. I wiped my mouth and tried again. Without even thinking about what I was going to play, I produced the first notes of a corny childhood ditty my aunt had taught me—

Christopher kneels at the foot of his bed

Lays on his little hands little gold head

—but I couldn't play more than the first two or three bars. The music moved me too much, the notes were intolerably sweet. I apologized to Dominique and the Indian—"I didn't play that, it was the flute"—the flute that had produced those sounds, so rich as to seem taboo.

You told me it was the same for you, Lili. You told me that when you played, your attention to the music had to be "floating," like that of a psychoanalyst, and that this destroyed your pleasure… but that if you were to listen, you'd run the risk of losing yourself in the beauty of each chord—

or slowing down, fascinated by your own fingers, in the middle of a *prestissimo*. Don't you remember? Oh Lili, where are you? Are you going to leave me even more alone than before? As it is there are so few of us, so very few.

VARIATIO XII: PEACE

Anonymous

She doesn't even breathe between the fragments. No one can tell, but she's wound up tighter than the strings of her harpsichord. I watched her tune it earlier. I'd arrived ahead of time. She was adjusting the length of every string with the tuning-key. First she checked the octaves and then the other intervals, to make sure their vibrations would coincide. She was alone in the room. She didn't know I was watching her. I saw her grow more and more tense. She was talking to herself: "That's not it, that's not it." Now and then she'd withdraw one of the quills and whittle it with a special blade, muttering over and over: "I'll never get it right." She stopped, adjusted her shoulders, and took a deep breath. Began again. When the lower manual was finally done, she compared it with the upper one. There was a slight difference between them; an almost imperceptible grating of the unison. This grating affected her as though it were physical pain—as though the quills were plucking not the strings of the instrument but her very nerves. Her frown deepened. Shortly after this, her husband came in and I went out onto the balcony. There were tables decked with bottles of chilled wine and platters of *petits four*. All of this suited her so badly.

I can't bear to know that she's unhappy. She reaches the end of each variation as though it were the end of an ordeal. She does all she can to conceal her effort, but I can see it. The way she keeps her hands on her knees, during the pause, as if to hide them. As if they'd just committed a crime. Sometimes she allows a good ten seconds to elapse, sometimes it's virtually *attaca*. But every time it seems like an attack: she returns to the ring for another round. And no one is there to wipe her forehead.

I'd like to go and take her by the hand—I'm sure her hands are cold—and lead her away from here, without a word. Would you come with me this time, Liliane? Your name is the only music we would need. You don't have to confront your demons in single-handed combat. We'd leave the room without a thought for the others. They'd stay behind, glued to their chairs, transfixed. We'd walk through the streets for a long while without speaking. I'd hold her only by the hand, not putting my arm around her waist. I'd make her sit down on a bench, I'd take her hands and rub them between mine. The stiffness of her fingers would gradually dissolve. She'd start to breathe again. I'd feel her opening, little by little, to the midsummer night. Remember, Liliane—there are stars, even in Paris. You'd forgotten. She'd look up at the sky and her white neck would stand out starkly against the shadow of the walls. She would shudder.

Come.

In my house, she'd walk like a somnambulist. In my house there is no music. The windows are always open onto the courtyard. We'd hear the noises of the night. Remember, Liliane—there are birds, even in Paris. A cricket now and then. I'd place my hands upon her shoulders. We'd remain thus, not moving, for a very long time, listening to the city birds. I'd speak to her of pigeons. How people despise them because they're so common, how they've become the cliché of every public square. And yet they used to be the birds of peace. They used to be called doves. Doves, Liliane—can you hear that word? And their love sounds are the same throughout the world. Coo coooo, coooo, coo coo. Always the identical scansion of their desire.

She wouldn't answer. I'd touch the nape of her neck beneath her hair. I'd feel the tendons tighten. I'd massage them very gently. She'd turn to me. She'd search out my eyes. Little by little, her own eyes would give in to the gentleness. I'd remain still until she'd finished looking at me. I wouldn't smile. I wouldn't speak. This would last a very long time. Nothing around us would change—the birds, the breeze. Finally, she would lift a hand. It would graze my hair. Her eyes would fill with sadness. No, Liliane—there's no reason to be sad. She'd whisper—yes, there is. She'd drop her eyes and press her forehead to my chest. She'd murmur, oh, your breathing is so calm—how can you be so very calm? I'd ease her down onto the sofa. I'd remove her sandals, take her feet between my hands and rub them—just as, earlier, I'd rubbed her hands. You're not afraid, Liliane. No, I'm not afraid of anything. That's a lie. Yes, that's a lie. You're not afraid of me. No. I'm not afraid of you.

She'd place both hands upon my head. We'd stay that way, again, for a very long time. Breathing. In my house there is no clock. Liliane doesn't wear a watch. The night would be eternal and unchanging—like the dovesong. Liliane would be naked by my side and I would be naked. Liliane would sniff my underarms, my groin and I would remain still. Liliane would sigh, almost moaning, and I'd say to her—I'm here. We're here, Liliane. She'd say—Yes. She'd stretch out on her back. I'd watch her chest rise and fall as she breathed. I'd place one hand on her stomach. She wouldn't close her eyes. We wouldn't say to each other—how beautiful you are. I'd lay my ear against her chest and listen to the beating of her heart. She'd put her arms around my shoulders like a crown of flowers. We'd remain thus, once again. Our nakedness would breathe.

Time wouldn't pass. Liliane and I would make love. I would penetrate her slowly. She wouldn't close her eyes. I'd see pearl drops of sweat forming on her forehead and upper lip. I'd place my lips against her lips to share this moisture. Inside her, I would be surrounded by her warmth, pressed by it. Liliane would place her hands on my hips, then on my buttocks. The slowness of our movements would be staggering. Our stomachs would seek each other out. There would be no more words at all—only noises, the enigmatic noises of human love. Liliane would be lying next to me and I would still be inside her. We'd look into each other's eyes. I'd see her opening up to the night and to herself, wider and wider, and tremble to see her like this at last—at last there would be no more fear anywhere. Liliane would press me to her. I'd go down into her depths, looking at her, loving her. The noises would descend further and further in her throat. At last there'd be the opening, the night embraced, the void so feared and so desired—and, flung beyond the edge of words, we'd scream to be these screaming bodies of which we knew nothing.

Liliane. Liliane and her harpsichord. Liliane Kulainn and her husband Bernald Thorer. It isn't true. You're lying to yourself. How much longer will you go on accepting these false constraints? How much longer must you pay your tithe of sadness? You claim to be blasé—because of all your failed loves and frazzled hopes. But these have nothing to do with you, and you know it. You're not this world-weary being you parody so well. You're not this "mature woman so touchingly like a child"—the years can't encroach upon you. You're not the daughter of a man whose name is Kulainn, nor the wife of a man whose name is Thorer. You are not the anything of anyone. *Liliane.* You're not even French like your mother, not even Irish like your father—you belong neither to a country nor a cause. You belong to nothing. I've been following you a very long time. You know that. You know I'm the only person in the world who loves what's really you.

On certain occasions, you've seen your own life through my eyes and found it senseless. You know you're betraying what you might be—making concessions, each and every day, of which you disapprove. The *petits four* on the balcony, the maidservant hired to welcome the guests, the string of pearls around your neck—these things are not you. Where are you hiding beneath it all, Liliane? And how much longer will you need to hide?

I'm waiting. Time does not exist. It ended the moment I met you. Since that day, there have been no more moments. There's been a space, and you know I'll always wait for you inside that space. I ask nothing of you. You'd never forgive me for asking. Only once did I ask you for something, and you consented—not to end our conversations on the phone with "Have a good day." You understand that you don't need to talk to me the way you talk to others. Your hostess's smile and artist's seduction are superfluous. You understand that my presence allows you to be silent—or else to seek, and to discover, different words. That's all I ask. That's what makes me know you believe in my love.

Fatigue is coming over you little by little. I can see it invading your whole body. You adjust your shoulders in defense, but it slips between your ribs and glides, reptile-like, the length of your backbone. Your limbs stiffen against it. You forget everything except that you must go on. You forget our years of sparsely scattered words. The shreds of your childhood which you tore away from the shadows to offer me. The gifts I've made you which have brought you joy. The stone exactly fitting the curve of your palm. The inhumanly perfect seashells.

Liliane, perfection is inhuman.

Haven't you learned that yet?

Liliane.

VARIATIO XIII: INSOMNIA

Franz Blau

In general her *tempi* are quite judiciously chosen, which is to say they're slower than those of other artists I might mention. This variation is perhaps a fraction too slow—but I much prefer that to the frenzied charge of a Glenn Gould. Someone had me listen to his version once, with nothing but good intentions, but even out of courtesy I was unable to bear it to the end. It was like galloping horses being whipped by a sadistic driver. Gould was constantly letting out grunts and groans of *Sturm und Drang*... whereas this piece was composed to bring peace to souls in search of slumber. In 1742, the year it was written, Bach was exactly my age. He understood Keyserlingk's request as no one else could have done. The progression of time signatures is calculated to perfection—3/4, 3/4, 2/4, 12/8, 3/8, 3/4, 3/8, 6/8, 3/4, 4/4, 2/2, 12/16, 3/4, 3/4, and so on—now two strong beats per measure and now three, but always the same pulsation, the same heartbeat from the first bar to the last. Bernald's wife has grasped that much, at least. Of course she's not a virtuoso like the young Goldberg himself; her execution is slightly flat and monotonous... The main thing, as every insomniac knows, is not to be rocked back and forth by the reiteration of the musical ideas, but rather to light the spark that allows you to short-circuit the current of conscious thought and plug into the wavelengths of the unconscious. *The Goldberg Variations* are admirably conceived to achieve this effect—each of them forms a separate imaginary universe, with its own coherence and its own laws. Here, for instance, in the thirteenth, there could be just the suggestion of a *rubato* after each dotted eighth note. And the trills shouldn't be executed identically from one variation to the next: it would be quite legitimate, now and then, to audibly prolong the auxiliary note, or accelerate to as many as six notes in the right hand against two in the left, instead of always settling for four to two. This should not be done systematically, of course. That's the main problem with Bernald's wife's technique—it's a bit too systematic, too conscientious. Her conception of classical music is relatively narrow: this has come out in all our conversations on the subject. For a musician, she shows surprising ignorance of whole epochs of musical history. Bernald's knowledge is infinitely more extensive than hers, though doubtless more superficial as well. For instance, whenever we broach the topic of opera, she turns mute. She claims to appreciate nothing but instrumental music—and, even within this category, she excludes the Romantics. When asked to be more specific, she replies vaguely, "the nineteenth century"—as though it were possible to dismiss Beethoven, Mendelssohn, Schubert, Schumann and Berlioz with a flip of the hand. Yet when asked whether she actually dislikes the Schubert *Lieder*, she admits she doesn't know them. Moreover, she's the victim of a deplorable fashion, always drawing analogies among the various arts. Thus, according to her, pre-nineteenth-century music corresponds to Gothic architecture, whereas Romantic music corresponds to Baroque architecture. Since she's never been an enthusiast of Baroque churches, she finds it natural to be allergic to opera. However, if Bernald and I point out that she appreciates Baroque music, she never fails to change the subject. Bernald has chosen a strange companion this time around. However, that doesn't worry me—I respect him enormously, and besides, I'm aware that to me any woman seen up close seems strange. With the exception of my own mother, of course—but then, when I met her, my faculty of judgment wasn't yet developed, so everything she did necessarily appeared normal. Indeed, it's highly likely that each individual's conception of normality derives from the ideal, all-embracing entity represented by the mother figure during childhood. My own mother was more corpulent than the average; consequently other women have always seemed underweight to me. My mother fed me potatoes three times a day, and even now a breakfast without *kartoffeln* feels incomplete. This obsessional character trait of mine did not go unnoticed by Bernald's wife. Today at noon the three of us were having lunch together; the new critic for *The Day* and his wife were also present. Bernald had made scalloped potatoes but the conversation led me to neglect them... We were talking about an *a capella* piece that had been discovered last year in Italy and attributed by some pseudo-experts to

Gesualdo. I got excited demonstrating the absolute inanity of this hypothesis; the *Day* critic attempted to counter me by suggesting that during a period of immaturity or lesser inspiration Gesualdo might indeed have stooped to composing something so mediocre. I got a bit carried away, and Bernald pointed out that it was unfortunate to let his cooking go to waste for the sake of a sheet of music four hundred years old, however debatable the latter figure might be. At this point I noticed the others had finished eating some time before, while my food had remained untouched. In order not to aggravate the impression of discourtesy this might have produced on the others by prolonging their wait, I ingurgitated the scalloped potatoes with unaccustomed haste. Bernald's wife burst out laughing—rather unkindly, I felt—"But Franz, you can't have been hungry, since you'd already eaten your dessert! No one was forcing you to finish the potatoes!" I joined in the general hilarity—people often find my absent-mindedness amusing—but they would probably not have understood had I attempted to explain that, where potatoes are concerned, I have no choice.

Mutti has been dead for almost twenty years now, but I'm still intensely aware of her presence in the kitchen. I haven't moved a thing: every object still occupies the place she once selected for it. I still put the napkins in the same drawer and the fruit in the same basket. When I return home after a day at the University, it's essential for me to find the kitchen in this order—as though we'd be having dinner together and nothing had changed. This is why I'm extremely reluctant to accept invitations to dine out: if by chance there were no potatoes on the menu, I'd feel as though I'd betrayed my mother. And since she's no longer around to scold me, the transgression of her rules gives me no pleasure whatsoever. I therefore far prefer to spend my evenings in my own library—just as I did when she was alive. She would always go to bed at half past ten, and I'd stay up a while longer, leafing through books in the silent apartment. Now, alas, the silence is not the same. Instead of protecting *Mutti*'s sleep, it reminds me brutally of her death. Towards one in the morning, I lose the capacity to concentrate on what I'm reading, and instead of growing drowsy I feel wider and wider awake. I begin to listen for her step in the hall, or her voice calling my name. Once I actually went into her room to make sure she wasn't there—wasn't in pain, in need of my help—I turned on the light, but of course her bed was empty.

When the silence gets too insistent, I go to the music room. It's windowless. I soundproofed both the walls and the doors myself, so as not to elicit complaints from my neighbours. I bring several scores with me from the library. They're interspersed among my books, arranged on the same shelves in chronological order. Living authors are in the hall... I can't resign myself to putting up shelves in Mutti's room. Carefully, I close the door to the music room. I pick out the record albums for the evening. On each cover is inscribed the optimal listening volume, as well as the predominance of bass and treble pitches. I settle down in my armchair, which is set up at an identical distance from each of the four loudspeakers. I open the first score to the first page. The music begins.

Since last spring, the records I've found most effective for inducing sleep have been the Mahler symphonies. Last year it was the *Nibelungen*. Sometimes I sense immediately that I've made the wrong choice, and change composers after listening only to one side. Most often I listen to at least eight or ten consecutive sides. Vivaldi's *Orlando Furioso*. The complete works of Alban Berg. By following the score, I strive to immerse myself in each master's particular genius. I can read several instruments at the same time—not always all of them, but at least those that are carrying the theme. I turn the pages as quickly as possible. The top right-hand corners are folded back slightly to make them easier to turn.

The music fills the room. It surrounds me as totally as if I myself were conducting it. Indeed, I sometimes find myself beating furiously on the arm of my chair as though it were a *maestro*'s music-stand.

When I finally emerge, exhausted, from the music room, the sky is already blanched with dawn. I return the scores to their shelves in the library, as well as the books I'd consulted earlier in the evening. I proceed to my room, which is at the end of the hall. The silence has been checkmated, my body pulverized by the music. If I can manage to prolong this sensation a few more minutes—just long enough to undress, put on my pyjamas, hang up my clothes in the wardrobe and brush my teeth—I'll be able to drop at last into a leaden slumber. *Schlaf' in himmlischer Ruh'*, my dear Keyserlingk.

The variation comes to a close with a divinely simple chord of thirds, announced by the E-flat of the left hand... Oh! A drop of *ritardando* wouldn't have done any harm.

VARIATIO XIV: TUMOUR

Olga

Their faces altered when they saw the wig, they couldn't help it. Bernald said nothing. Liliane said, "It suits you beautifully!" right away. Lies. More lies. Are people going to keep on lying to me until the end of my life? Yes. All of them. "You're not eating enough, Olga. You're thinner every time I see you. Come on, have some chocolates, have some peanuts, have some of these cookies—I baked them just for you." Lies. I eat more than I've ever eaten in my life. At the clinic they'd bring me a tray every four hours and I'd gulp down everything on it—fat, gravy, mashed potatoes, bread and butter—my appetite's never been so good. "You must come and relax with us in the country, Mother. You'll get well faster. The children are looking forward to your visit." Lies. The children don't give a shit and neither do I. I'll do what I feel like doing. I've always hated the country, so don't use that to assuage your guilty conscience. Think up something else. Use your imagination. I'll go where I feel like going. "Darling, tell me what I can bring you. Anything. The price doesn't matter." Lies. The price you'd pay to buy off your cruelty matters a lot to you. And I'm not your darling—no more now than during our fifteen years together.

It's disgusting the way hypocrisy oozes out as soon as death enters the picture. Like worms that suddenly materialize in meat, secreted by the very flesh you were about to consume. Oh, no. I'm not going to efface myself anymore; it's my turn to play the egotist. Leave me alone. For Christ's sake, you've never done anything but that! I want to think about myself. I've a certain number of accounts to settle with my lousy life.

Bernald must have been surprised to hear me talk that way when he came to the clinic last week. My hair was falling out by the handful and I didn't have the wig yet. I looked hideous. He, at least, didn't fuck me over by telling me I looked ravishing. He's the only one who hasn't fucked me over, all these years. Very rare bird, a former lover who doesn't stab you in the back. So I told him, "Listen carefully, Sonny. Mamma's gonna teach you the facts of life." And he listened. I told him how glad I was. Don't you realize? I'm completely free. I don't owe anyone anything. I don't have to look pretty anymore; I don't even look at myself in the mirror. I don't have to play the wife anymore—or the mother, or the grandmother—I'm nothing but a corpse-to-be. They're all shitting in their frocks. It scares them to see me like this. At last I'm revolting. I can use dirty language. I can insult everyone and they'll chalk it up to my illness. They want to hang on to their happy memories of me—smiling Olga, submissive Olga, self-sacrificing Olga. But I'm going to smash those memories to bits. There's still time.

Bernald started blubbering. He cries a lot these days. But at least I could tell that his weren't tears of pity. I spit on those. I could tell he understood what I was trying to say. I started blubbering, too. "What a relief!" I said. "Believe me, Bernald, it's a relief for me to kick the bucket. Even if I'm in pain, it's wonderful to know I've only got a month or two to go. I won't have to drag this lousy life all the way to senility, and I won't be struck down without warning by a heart attack, either. Do you understand? It's wonderful. It's as if a veil had suddenly lifted. For the past fifty years I've been wandering through this sort of murky cloud, and finally I'm going to emerge. I've had one motherfucker of a life, Bernald. I'm glad to get out of it—honestly."

Bernald's the only one who understands I'm not complaining for the sake of complaining. I've never complained—never. Never. After all, they might try listening, if only for the novelty of it. Instead of blaming it on the decay of my brain cells. I've never complained! And boy, do I resent it. I resent everyone, including myself...but especially you, you who've started calling me darling now for the first time since we were married. I resent you for having sat across the table from me in silence. I resent you for having acted as though my son didn't exist. I resent your violent displays of jealousy. You made my life even more hellish than it was before I met you. Of course I was less than nothing at the time, a waitress turning tricks to make ends meet. Of course you initiated me into the joys of big money, took me to exotic countries, introduced me to all your TV and movie star friends. Fuck. Once at home, between the two of us, what was there?

Whisky. Yeah. We had a lot of talent for getting pissed together. There was plenty of whisky between us. What else?

Your Dickinson grand piano. Your Dick, as you called it, with your usual good taste, to get a laugh out of our guests. They'd ask you to play something. "Come on, don't be modest." Ha! You, modest? You didn't make them ask twice. Four or five preludes and fugues, played with "divine simplicity." Have I got it right? Those same preludes and fugues which I had drummed into me from morning to night. Whenever you were the least bit depressed you'd clam up completely, not a word for me, no way I could comfort you, I'd ceased to exist—ah, but your Dick was there, and you'd spend hours and hours and hours pouring out your troubles to it. I'd sit in the bedroom trying to read, trying not to go off my rocker. You didn't want me to talk on the phone—it disturbed you. You didn't want me to work—that disturbed you, too. As far as you were concerned, any woman who worked was a bit of a tramp—and since I'd already had a taste of the real thing…

You never let me forget that, either. You'd bring it up every time you got drunk, even in front of other people. "Olga, you know how to hustle, go hustle us up some ice cubes, won't you, baby?" Every time you fucked me, too. You'd call me bitch, whore. You knew what you were talking about—you'd been with lots of them in Korea. When I first met you, you didn't even take your pants off to fuck, just dropped them to your knees. That was your Don Juan technique—hit and run.

Once I'd taught you how to make love, you couldn't wait to try out all the new positions on other women. At first I was devastated. Girls would call you up at home. I'd say, "It's for you" and go off and blubber in the bedroom so as not to disturb you. After a while I got used to it; I didn't give a shit. I decided if I couldn't work, I could at least get some education. I registered at the University. You made fun of me. I took all kinds of courses. It was exciting; at least it got me out of the house. That's how I met Bernald—I sat in on his seminar and found it fascinating, just as everyone else did. I never dreamed he'd pay any attention to me. But he did—one day we had coffee together after class, he asked me a lot of questions, he listened to me the way you never had. When I came home that night, I wanted to put a bullet through my head. You weren't home. You came in at four in the morning, dead drunk. I was waiting up for you. You didn't even say hi; you fell into bed. I went out, I couldn't stand it anymore. I walked through the streets at random, I went into a bar, I had a drink. When I came out a guy started following me. He crushed me against a wall, said he was going to rape me, called me all the names you call me, whore, bitch, you're going to get it, my fat prick, that's what you're asking for. I screamed until I thought my lungs would tear and he finally took to his heels. Not a single window opened, not a single cop appeared. I went home—in pieces. The next day I told you what had happened. I was blubbering. I told you I wanted to die. You said don't be silly; if he'd raped you I'd understand your killing yourself, but he didn't even touch you.

For me that was the end. It was only then I started taking lovers. You went mad with rage when you found out I was sleeping with Bernald. You bellowed at me day and night. You forbade me to use the telephone at all. You fucked me as brutally as possible. You tweaked my nipples till I screamed and begged for mercy. One day you announced you were going to assassinate Bernald in the middle of his seminar. You would have done it, too. I stopped going. I stayed in the apartment. Preludes and fugues, preludes and fugues, more relentlessly than ever. Bach. Bach. Bach.

Now, it's true, you've had the piano moved down to the house in Florida. Perhaps you wanted to make room for my coffin? I know you pay a phenomenal amount of money to keep the humidity constant inside the house—otherwise your Dick would suffer. Ocean air is very bad for Dicks. The wood starts mouldering, the strings go limp and have to be adjusted every couple of weeks. So you did that just for me? How touching. You're spending all that money so I can finally have some peace and quiet in our home? How sweet of you. I hope your Dick rots before I do.

You even let me go out alone at night now, to visit old friends. "Whatever you want, darling. It won't disturb me if you see Bernald." Now that I'm nothing but a rag full of holes. Now that my little birdbrain has exploded. I can make lots and lots of phone calls. I can register at all the universities in the world.

I've made a mess of my life. It's revolting. But I'm not going to make a mess of my death. I'm going to die my way.

I want to be burned. I want my ashes to be scattered in the Gulf of Mexico. That way you won't be able to come to my tombstone once a year and sniffle as you tell my grandchildren the tale of Gramma's life. My life is a pile of shit. There's nothing to tell. Nothing to salvage. I've wasted my time.

VARIATIO XV: SOFTSTONE

Bernald Thorer

This, you've told me, is the Variation you love most of all—perhaps, indeed, the only one you truly love. Because of its *chromaticism*, that lovely word which bespeaks colour: the careful shadings of its notes; the phrases tranquilly ascending and descending the scale of G minor by half-steps. *Chroma* also means the skin—through what semantic association? You display to us these variegated skins, the successive surfaces of something with no core. For what the variations repeat is not the melody of the theme, but the organisation of its harmonies. There is no progression towards a climax, no revelation of an ultimate meaning—there could be a thousand variations, couldn't there?—and the empty centre would remain the same.

Outside, the wind has risen. Inside, the guests seem wary and a little tense. They wonder what they're doing here. They suspect you had some ulterior motive for giving this concert. It's as though they'd suddenly found themselves upon a stage, without the slightest idea what play they were in or which role they'd been assigned. Does anyone have the key? Is anyone going to prompt them? Not that what's going

on is outright abnormal—after all, they're just attending a
chamber music concert in Paris in the month of June—yet
the malaise is there, there's no getting around it. The strange
pomp with which you've surrounded the performance. Your
black dress, the candlelight, your Irish cousin dressed up as a
maid, the plates of food on the balcony—all this must correspond to a particular convention, yet they can't quite figure
out which. On the one hand, the concert began at "precisely
eight o'clock," which makes it sound like a serious musical
event, but on the other hand, there are refreshments, so afterwards they'll have to tune up for a society function. It gets
them confused, the symbols are contradictory, it's neither one
nor the other yet both at once—how will they hit on the
right tone?…

And what is this concert for, in the first place? For nothing, of course—music is always for nothing. Music has no
raison d'être; no reason whatsoever—this is why the French
find it so bewildering. This evening, you decided to drop
emphatic hints here and there—as if to imply that it was
possible to discover an interpretive path and follow it somewhere. You chose the 24th of June, the night of the Saint-
Jean, the night of enchantment. You sought to draw them
into a sort of midsummer night's dream. But they don't
want to get drawn in. They keep looking for the key to the
mystery, the interpretation of the dream. Each guest is
acquainted with only a few of the others; the gathering is
neither intimate enough nor impersonal enough for them
to know what foot to stand on. So they're suspending their

judgment—you can sense it and it makes you nervous. But you'll see—it doesn't matter. Or rather—this concert matters enormously and not at all; every note is simultaneously gratuitous and absolutely necessary. These *Goldberg Variations* didn't need to exist in the first place, but once they had begun to exist, they had no choice but to take on a particular form and become it utterly.

When I was a writer, I would constantly encounter the same dilemma. I was so anxious not to build walls but latticework constructions with my words that I dreaded falling through the openings I myself had shaped. You talked to me about doors that could be neither open nor closed—do you remember?—but "ajar," and we tried to imagine an alternative to both the excessively Western penchant for filling things up and the excessively Eastern one for emptying them out. But I was convinced, and still am, that writing is incapable of illustrating this alternative (at least here and now); that it will always be full to overflowing; that it cannot help but be transformed into a discipline—did you know Blanchot and Duras are now on the high school curriculum? …Music, though, has a better chance, since it's non-didactic; permeability is its very essence. Meaning is hard as a rock, but music is porous like soapstone—or like those volcanic stones we picked up on the beach in Italy. Once they'd been smouldering lava; now the sea washed freely through their cavities. They were solid and empty at the same time. Will you enjoy this image? I'll give it to you tomorrow—perhaps you'll be able to turn it into a smile or a haiku…

As you were practising these past weeks, I marvelled constantly—don't worry, I won't say at your talent—at the process itself; the crafting of a masterpiece. The fragments being gradually aligned and polished, then finally coalescing in a current. The technical aspect of beauty is always a mystery. When I listen to birdsong, I can content myself with knowing it's instinctive—nothing is less enigmatic than nature. But when I listen to a madrigal, I know that the person singing it had to learn things called slurs, tremolos, *pincés*, trills, glides, mordents, accidentals—and I'm overcome with admiration. So much precision in order to say nothing.

Now you've reached the middle of the concert. You're tired, and I know how much you hate fatigue. You told me once that you needed to keep your eyes open—*like* wounds. You felt that you had to represent the "neither open nor shut" with your own body; to let yourself be "flayed" by your contact with life. You don't use that word anymore...but I'll never forget the day you returned from an art exhibit, white as a sheet, and informed me that an unknown painter had given a shape to your obsession. The painting showed a man leaping out of a refrigerator: he was naked, skeletal, frozen in mid-air as though electrified; his hair stood on end, his genitals drooped, his skin was red with bluish patches..."The Flayed One"—a frightening image, but also the image of fright itself. I asked you whether Christ crucified didn't reflect exactly the same fantasy—an emaciated, youthful body, drenched with sweat and blood, in front of which millions of worshippers had bowed or knelt—I suggested you might recognize yourself in this exacerbated sensitivity, this need to be virtually raw—"Gaze upon my wounds, all ye who doubt; put your hand into the gash. For you have I suffered; for you I suffer still"—you were angry with me for days. Perhaps I was wrong… As I watch you now, I can see there's something else at stake. I can sense you using your fatigue; using the constraints instead of fighting them.

During our stay at your grandmother's place in Ireland, you slept nine hours a night. I couldn't believe it—your face in the morning was totally at peace, and during the day you never rushed—you'd adopted the calm slowness of your grandmother. I watched you going over to the well, drawing water, cutting sprigs of mint and making tea, and I realized that beneath its usual Parisian rhythm, your body had a different, less erratic beat—less powerful, too, perhaps, but more assured. That is the beat I can hear in this concert; you're beginning to place your trust in it. So never mind whether people are listening or not. Olga is listening. So are Franz—and Simon—and Jules, of course. Viviane can't take her eyes off you—there's another "Flayed One." Your father has almost completely swivelled around in his chair, but he's listening in his own way; all of them are listening in their own way and so am I and so are you. The malaise is due less to the Variations than to the people, whose simultaneous presence in this room is as much a part of the performance as the music itself. And since each of these lives is also a facet of yours or mine, the sum total is complex and unwieldy.

Perhaps when it's all over, you won't feel like mingling with the guests right away. Perhaps we could duck out and let them look after the casting of the play? Who is to be the hero, who the heroine and who the oracle? Who will sing in the chorus and who will dance in the coryphaeus? Will supper be the epilogue of the concert, or was the concert the prologue to the supper? Meanwhile, we'll take a walk in the garden. The full moon will have risen. From below, we'll glance up at the guests on the balcony. Their words will be muffled by the time they reach our ears—like a chaotic piece of music, the anti-concert, as it were, during which they can release what they've been holding back for one and a half hours. We'll hear false laughter and real laughter, false questions and real ones, while distinguishing nothing but the inflections—the punctuation of the utterances and not their content—some of them entirely in parentheses and others entirely in quotes, some sprinkled with exclamation marks and others with question marks or ellipses…

Now I remember why it is you love this fifteenth variation more than all the rest: instead of resolving on the tonic, it prolongs its questioning with three notes from the right hand—three notes still rising up to the unknown?

VARIATIO XVI: PROFIT

Sylvère Laurent

There was the fixed-price meal for the four of us, plus two bottles of Morgan, plus the coffee; even if the Morgan did cost a bit more than what was marked on the wine list, I can't figure out how they reached a total of 578 francs, with the meals at only 80 francs apiece. Of course I could put it on my expense account, but that would be my the fourth business lunch this week and I don't like to set such a bad example. But then, it's not as though anybody's keeping track. For the accountant's office, these are negligible sums. Still, I don't like to do it. I tell Marilyn to take a pocket calculator along when she goes to the supermarket... What I saw out there on the balcony most definitely did not come from a supermarket. More like Fauchon's. Unless their little maid has an exceptional gift for fancy snacks. I think I saw some cucumber sandwiches—maybe she's British? But then, maybe she was just hired for the evening. Liliane Kulainn probably earns a decent salary at UNESCO, but I doubt she's rolling in wealth. Her father's here—she introduced us before the concert—and he hardly looks like a Lord. Are the Irish even eligible for nobility? Sir James Joyce? Sounds weird. Sir Samuel Beckett? Pretty unlikely. Be that as it may, I see that Lady Kulainn is wearing a pearl necklace this evening. And even with his royalties, Thorer can't possibly afford to give presents like that. More likely she's supporting him these days. Funny thing. Thorer was well on his way to becoming a rich man. If he'd been a bit more careful about his contracts with foreign publishers, instead of flaunting that famous indifference of his—virtually his personal trademark up to the time of his nervous breakdown—he would have been guaranteed a more than comfortable retirement. Not that he looks uncomfortable as things are, but I doubt it's much fun to be a kept man.

His depression took the wind out of his sails; it is a shame. There was a sentence that characterized him perfectly, in a book review published by *The Day* two or three years ago— how did it go? Something like—"Whereas most contemporary thinkers strive to seem nonchalantly intelligent, only Bernald Thorer manages to be intelligently nonchalant." It was phrased a bit better than that, but that was basically it. His illness has really transformed him. He looks more serious than before, but also more ethereal. Must have lost a pound or two. It was really impressive. Never seen anything like it. Of course we managed to play it down, for the sake of his reading public, but it really blew me away. I'd been following his career from afar for something like twenty years. It seemed to me we had a lot in common. Both of us were ambitious, both of us had high ideals and an unlimited amount of energy to put into them. Both of us had been A students—we graduated from university the same year, got our doctorates the same year, had our first taste of success when we were still practically kids. By the time we turned thirty, we'd made a name for ourselves. When I decided to start *The Other Day*, I even took Thorer out to lunch and asked him to write a weekly column for it. Offered him five thousand francs a month—not bad for as many words. But he turned me down—very politely, of course—saying he'd prefer just to send me an article from time to time, whenever an idea occurred to him, rather than receive a regular salary. Not that *The Other Day* could have guaranteed him a living—as it turned out, it was more like the other way around; his name might have helped *The Other Day* survive... In short, it wasn't a very fruitful encounter.

Then—when, exactly?—I was already working for *The Day*, so it must have been a year or two later, the rumour started circulating that Thorer had gone crazy. I just refused to believe it. I thought—must be the classic mid-life crisis. A bit early, maybe—but then, Bernald Thorer always was precocious. Everyone has the right to feel shaky on his feet once in a while. All we've got to do is act supportive, keep telling him that what he writes really matters to us, that we're in desperate need of his oh-so-original ideas, and so on—and wait for the whole thing to blow over.

This was right around the time Vietnam invaded Cambodia—people were starting to hear about all the atrocities that had been committed under Pol Pot. I figured it might be a good idea to do a "Forum" on the subject in *The Day*, so I solicited an article from Bernald Thorer. Just to get him cogitating again, about something other than his depression. I waited and waited, the article didn't come, but every time my secretary rang him up he'd say it was on its way, he just needed a while longer to think it over... We postponed that "Forum" for two whole weeks; I started bitching about writers having no idea what was meant by current events—the situation in Cambodia had already changed and I was getting seriously pissed off. Finally, one day I come into my office, I find an envelope on my desk with Bernald Thorer's name on the back. So I open it up and what do I find?—a single sheet of paper. I thought it must be a bad joke. There was practically nothing on it, just a few words scattered here and there: "It's horrible," "NO," "It's————"; there were other words that weren't even legible, plus a few comic-strip onomatopoeia, "Aaaaargh" and the like. I said to myself, "Where does this guy get off?" Boy, was I furious. I decided that was the last time I'd try doing Bernald Thorer a favour. The "Forum" came out the next day—without his contribution, of course.

I still didn't realize how serious his illness was. I didn't tell anyone but Marilyn about the unpublished letter. She said she found it more intelligent that the articles we'd published. Very funny. I waited to see what would happen to the *enfant terrible* who'd suddenly regressed to the stage of an *enfant sauvage*. Had he actually lost the use of the French language? Apparently not. Some of the friends we had in common still saw him from time to time; according to them, Thorer had lost none of his usual deference—he was a bit more absent-minded than before, but there was nothing dramatic about his condition.

The television scandal came shortly after that, and marked the end of his career. He'd been invited to a talk show to present his most recent book, about the ideologies of war. The other guests were historians and philosophers who'd approached the same topic from other angles—they'd even dug up an ex-Legionnaire who'd just published his memoirs, to spice the evening up a bit—but the whole thing was like a gift in gratitude to Bernald Thorer, or at least a vote of confidence. The host questioned the other guests first—partly to keep Thorer for the *pièce de résistance*, but also as an indication of the high esteem in which he was held. So the others spoke in turn, quarreling a bit the way they always do, just to make things interesting, and Thorer's total silence grew more and more conspicuous, not to say insolent. The camera scanned his face from time to time—he was paying close attention to what the others were saying, but not making the least attempt to intervene. At last the host turned to him and said, "What about you, Bernald Thorer—what do you think? Are we headed for Apocalypse?" Thorer hesitated, then blurted out, "I wholeheartedly agree with Mr. Benoit," and fell silent once again. A dreadful hush came over the whole studio. Now, silence is a very expensive thing on TV. Poor Benoit turned green at the gills. Even the host, there to keep the discussion moving no matter what, was struck dumb.

That sentence was destined to become Bernald Thorer's most famous quote. It was repeated incredulously in every university corridor throughout Paris and the provinces; it was whispered in publishing houses for fully three months. After that, Thorer had no choice but to withdraw from the public stage once and for all. You can't just go and thumb your nose at the institutions that have been sponsoring and encouraging you for years. He'd agreed to appear on TV, and then he'd pulled a fast one on them... or rather a slow one, like zero miles an hour. Well, if that was what he wanted...

This evening he welcomed me very naturally. I hadn't talked to him since the Cambodia affair—but I'm not mad anymore, of course. I pity him, is more like it. He told me he still reads *The Day*—not every day, but every "other day"—so I guess he hasn't turned into a total hermit. Still, I pity him. He was well on his way to having an extraordinary career. We'd tried out our wings together, so to speak, and I'd had the feeling we were supporting each other from afar, with a sort of tacit comradeship. Now he acts as though he's quite detached from all that—which doesn't prevent him from being a failure, in my eyes; I still think it's a real shame.

VARIATIO XVII: CARES

Irène Serino

I'm almost sure I turned it off—how stupid to be thinking about that. Like when I was a student and I had to get up at six in the morning to do my exercises, I'd wind the clock but then I'd wonder if I hadn't forgotten to set the alarm. I'd get out of bed to check and of course it would always be set—I never forgot anything in those days. As a matter of fact I used to wish I could forget things. It worried me that I never made the slightest Freudian slip. I thought I must be abnormal, I must be the only one without an unconscious. Now it's different—I forget something every day. Jules would get after me about it, if it weren't for the fact that he's even worse. I could never leave him alone with the children, for example. He'd forget to give them their baths; he might even forget to feed them. But it's not the same kind of forgetfulness…he could lock himself up in his studio for a week, without washing and virtually without eating—his family would cease to exist. He doesn't realize everyone isn't like him.

Did I turn it off or didn't I? Oh, dear. I remember taking the car keys from the dresser drawer right next to the lamp; ordinarily I would have switched it off then, before leaving the room. But I have no recollection of crossing the room in the dark. How silly, there's no reason why it should catch fire—we leave it on while we're in the house and it hasn't happened yet. But that lampshade... unbleached wool is highly inflammable... and the curtains right beside it... they'd have time to ignite before the children knew anything was happening, since all of them sleep upstairs now. The carpet, then the furniture, then the walls...the staircase...the smoke rising, infiltrating...the whole house could go up... I mustn't think about it. I'm sure I turned it off. And even if I did forget, Sandra will have noticed it before going to bed. She knows I tend to worry. "Don't be silly, Mom, we're old enough now. You let me babysit for your friends, so why don't you trust me here? Everyone will be in bed on time, I promise." It's five to nine, so they're probably all asleep by now. Sandra is very responsible. I know I can trust her. In fact the other night I dreamed we were on a beach together and the tidal wave was rising—she was the one who saved me from the sea.

I often have nightmares when Jules is working nights. I know he's right next door, but I still have the same fears as when I was little—I've always hated falling asleep alone. It's so much nicer when we go to bed together and talk about what we've done during the day, the children, their school-work, the friends we'll be having over for Saturday dinner. When I'm alone, I don't think much about anything, as a matter of fact. Or just silly things that go through my head, I wonder if the boys have enough clean socks or if I should do the wash tomorrow. Or else I try to remember, in order, all the pupils I've seen during the day.

Today Mischa had her lesson—she's really got talent, but is she ever touchy! She wants to study with me but she can't stand the slightest criticism. "Last week you told me my touch should be firmer, this week you tell me to relax. I can't do both at once!" She's got some nerve, talking to me that way, even if her father's name is Grinski. After all, I don't get paid for listening to that sort of impertinence, but for shaping artists.

Thirty-two pupils this year—four more than last year, whereas I swore I was going to cut down on my teaching activities— that's really too many. I hardly have time for my own practising. We're giving a concert in two weeks and all we've done is sight-read through the music once together. It's not going to be a breeze, either—this Evangelisti guy and his "Aleatory Music." It's going to take us at least two hours a page just to get our respective entries right. Jules says that's what makes contemporary music so interesting—every composer invents a totally new system of notation. Which is all right with me, except that I wasn't trained that way. It's like new math—I can't help the boys with their homework because nothing even vaguely resembles what I was taught. I used to really enjoy math, too, when I was in high school. I hesitated a long time between math and music. My parents are the ones who wanted me to do music—they said it was more feminine. I'm not even sure I was right to follow their advice. Sometimes I think I might have had a gift for mathematical research... But the *Jeunesses musicales* are what made up my mind: nothing in the world is more exalting than to sit in the midst of a symphony orchestra, feel the music blossoming into life all around you, and know you're a part of that blossoming. Then you feel you really belong—whereas math is a solitary practise.

On the other hand, orchestra musicians are anonymous, almost by definition. So when I joined the quartet ten years ago, I thought I'd found the ideal solution. Unfortunately, it's anything but lucrative, so I have to waste my time giving lessons just like everybody else. I contribute more to the family budget than Jules does—but everybody finds that natural, since composers are more "artistic" than performers. People get all excited when they come over for dinner; they bombard Jules with questions, then they turn to me and ask politely, "And what do you do?"—and when I tell them I'm a violinist they don't expect me to have anything to add. I don't see why they automatically assume that he has opinions about music and I don't. Still, it's true we're not the same... Sometimes I watch him when he gets talking about it—I can see how engrossed he is, how completely impassioned—and it saddens me. I know it isn't fair. But I used to be impassioned, too—especially when I was young and starting to discover the violin repertory for the first time. The years of practise and preparation had brought my talent to fruition: I felt capable of mastering even the most difficult pieces. And sometimes I got quite carried away... It's been a long time since I've felt that way. Even during concerts, my soul almost never takes flight anymore. I don't know...you see that sort of ecstasy more often on men's faces than on women's. When Jules is conducting, for example, the expressions on his face are exactly the same as when we make love. This really gets to me, because I'd already noticed it with other musicians. I've seen I don't know how many violinists and cellists twisting their features into an expression of exquisite pain, like that of sexual pleasure. If they didn't have the pretext of their instruments, they'd never dare do that in public. At least Jules has his back turned to the audience—thank goodness. The way men get involved in music is too intimate, too physiological for my taste. A couple of weeks ago, we went to hear Frédéric Dumont—Jules often draws on jazz for inspiration. Dumont's face was so contorted, you would have thought he was making love to his saxophone. His whole body was writhing...honestly. I've never seen a woman do that. Look at Liliane—she's like a statue when she plays. I could never let myself go that way, either. There's always a distance between me and my instrument; it never becomes like an organ of my own body. When Jules starts writing something, it's as if music took the place of his entire body. That's why he doesn't need to wash or eat. I'm not jealous of the time he devotes to his music—better that than a mistress—but sometimes I get jealous of his involvement with it. After all, it is my profession, too.

Once I even tried to talk it over with him. I asked him why, in his opinion, there were so few women composers. He said it was obvious—having been kept in the house and saddled with kids, women had never had access to a serious musical education. Now that they've been emancipated, he went on, more and more of them will become composers. Maybe even our Sandra someday—who knows? That sounds like a likely explanation, but I don't know... I feel as if it were only part of the truth. Will there really be a woman composer as great as Beethoven some day? Or a woman conductor of the stature of von Karajan? I doubt it, but I'm not sure why. Still, you can't predict the future. Next month, as a matter of fact, we'll be meeting one of the up-and-coming women composers at the Berkshire Festival. An American—I can't remember her name, but apparently she's a real tyrant. She invariably conducts her own symphonies, and forces her musicians to rehearse until they drop. It'll be fun to see that, just the two of us. The first time we'll have taken a trip alone together since our honeymoon. Sandra will be on a linguistic exchange program in London, and the boys at summer camp. Between now and then I'll have to find the time to sew on their name tags. One for every pair of underpants, one for every sock, one for every T-shirt... that'll make at least sixty altogether. If each tag takes me three or four minutes, it's going to occupy a full evening. Not tomorrow evening, though,

VARIATIO XVIII: SYNCOPE

Jules Serino

…her search for authenticity. Makes me laugh. Doesn't like being teased. Goes off and sulks in a corner. Makes you want to laugh even more. So she's got a harpsichord just like the ones they used to make in such-and-such a year in such-and-such a town in Italy. So what? Her suspiciousness of everything modern. Putting down living artists and craftsmen—why? Just because they're alive. Bach is nice. I have no trouble admitting the old stuff is nice. What have they got against the new stuff? I know. It doesn't lull them to sleep. It keeps jerking them awake. Over and over. Every second. It's too much. People prefer to sleep. I've always known that. Even when I was a kid. Terrible. Nodding off in the metro. In the street. In front of the TV set. Around the dinner table. Turn on the radio. The record player. Fall more deeply asleep. Yoga. Jogging. Movies. They get nervous—it's a tragedy. So they've got nerves? Neuroses? No sweat—quick, a tranquillizer! Let's droop a little more. Droop until we drop—hard drugs, if necessary. Comfortable furniture. Cozy cushions. Dark glasses. Rock 'n roll. Move your body any which way. Sing your own thing. Return to nature. What nature? For example: return to ancient instruments. Are they natural? What a joke. They know all about the times they live in: nuclear plants, oil spills, massacres, destruction. Creation? Whazzat? Creation was before. Before what? Before capitalism. Completely off their rockers.

I like teasing Lili. "Why don't you like contemporary music?" "I do—I like Schoenberg." That's what she calls contemporary. Good old Arnold kicked the bucket half a century ago. I play his Opus 26 for her, the string quintet. "There—I feel as if I'm being invited to listen, instead of being excluded." People with high IQ's talking like that. They visit art museums and go into ecstasy over Pollock. But they don't want their ears to work. As it is, their grey matter has to work, and their eyes, and their hands. Enough, already. You can't expect more than that. If listening to music means work, what's the world coming to? Music is for killing time. Everyone knows that. Not for bringing time to life. Take disco. Now, that's interesting. Time reduced to mush. At last you can't hear a thing. But today's composers. Too cold, too intellectual. Conceptual music, what a drag. As though their flatulent Sibelius was anything else. Different concepts, that's all. But they get scared. Don't like the idea of electronics. Makes them think of *1984*. Or Watergate. The cold calculations of the cold machine. You shouldn't mix science and art. As though their well-tempered harpsichord was anything else. A different science, that's all. The synthesizer is a fabulous invention. Pure science fiction. It scares them. It can imitate to perfection not only every instrument that exists, but an infinite number of instruments that don't.

Instruments impossible to make. It just isn't natural. The flute, the clarinet, the violin, the saxophone—those are natural. And why should the number of fingers we happen to have on our two superior-primate hands limit our musical possibilities? After all, we stopped counting on them long ago! Well yes, it is useful to know how to multiply. It is helpful to calculate one's taxes on the computer. But music? Untouchable. You can't trust a synthesizer. In the first place, it's heavy. In the second place, it's complicated. In the third place, it's expensive. Antisocial. So we won't have anything to do with it. Take it away. Nothing but noise. You can't use it for begging in cinema line-ups like you can a guitar. So it's not spontaneous. Not a bird on the wing.

OK, let's see what we have in the way of birds. Our great, "spontaneous" opera soloists. The soprano misses her high A in the recording session. What do you do about it? Can't let it pass. So the record is a write-off? No way—that's where the synthesizer comes in. Minor surgery on the A: it gets squeezed up a quarter-tone. Face-lift, as it were. Now it's beautiful, now it's aesthetic. Bravo! Long live science? Not on your life— long live the soprano!

So the composers. Poor guys. Do what they can. Try to put people at ease. Give them renovated folklore. Quotations from music they already dig. Bits of poetry to help it go down better. Sugar coating on the pill. I'm no better—I write for the movies. Glue my sounds to images—maybe that way they won't notice. Contemporary music gets slipped into films like arsenic into tea. Or like invisible advertising. Flash: "Buy popcorn." Flash: "Listen to Serino." They hear without listening. Sometimes it works. At least I get royalties.

Sounds in silence. Sounds in space. I never use the piano. I use infinity. People raise their eyebrows. For them, the keyboard is like the alphabet. Isn't that enough for you? Eighty-eight notes—whereas there are only twenty-six letters, and the poets have never complained. What if I want a quarter-tone? An eighth of a tone? Five-ninths of a tone? What if I want exactly that? It's like honeydew melons. God divided them into six slices for the express purpose of being eaten by large families. Major and minor modes are a gift of God. Perfectly adapted to our auditory system. The rest is nothing but noise. Grating of nerves, grinding of teeth. Like when I told Lili there were electric harpsichords on the market. What a face she made! Nose turned up in disgust. Bernald shows a bit more interest. He asks questions. Hasn't made up his mind about everything in advance. Most people have their minds made up by the time they climb out of the cradle. What they want is to be rocked. Take a seventy-year nap. But they realize they've got to have taste. Know what they like and what they hate. Be individuals. That is: learn what's considered good taste. Then say you like it. Say everything else is disgusting. Bernald isn't like that. He had a ball with my Japanese gadget. Held the perforated cards against the light. Tried to guess the composer by looking at the design made by the holes. Then slid it into the machine. Got a real kick out of making music by turning a handle. Like an old-fashioned coffee mill. Same idea as player pianos or organ-grinders, except it's no bigger than a wallet. Bernald's like me, he loves toys. So first he runs through a Bach Invention. We listen to it four times. Beginning to end. End to beginning. Then you turn the card over. Inversion: beginning to end, end to beginning. That made four Bach Inventions. Lili pretended to be reading. She wondered if we weren't doing something sacrilegious. We took Mozart. Turned him upside-down. In the fourth position, it almost sounded like something modern. Bernald's mouth was hanging open. We took Beethoven. It turned into mush, as could only be expected. Lili got up with this triumphant look on her face. That proves Bach is the best of the lot! The most authentic! Since every which way sounds the right way up.

People are addicted to the right way up. It reassures them. They can't bear the world being stood on its head. An Invention that sounds the same four times in a row is good. A truly inventive Invention? Just try it. So I do—I take out a fresh card. Pick up the little hole-puncher. Compose a piece before their very eyes. Don't write a thing. Just punch holes. Like they used to do for metro tickets. I work fast. Holes at the top of the card, then at the bottom, then a vertical line of holes in the middle. Intervals that could never be played simultaneously on the piano. Then cascades of quarter-tones. Then long silences. I hand them the card. I know what it's going to sound like. I can hear it just by looking at it. Bernald is enjoying himself. Lili isn't. The whole thing's too arbitrary. There's nothing for her to latch onto. I run the card through backwards. Lili gets bored. Goes and fixes herself a drink. Alcohol. More sleep. Lights a cigarette. I object. More drugs. I get a bit carried away and call her a degenerate. She starts to laugh. Condescendingly. As if to say: little Jules is going to throw his temper tantrum. He may be brilliant but boy is he naïve. Let's try to explain things to him. "It's not so much the melody I miss," she says. "I don't insist on having tunes I can whistle." How evolved can you get? "I think it's the rhythm. Perhaps because the body has its own, authentic rhythm. The heart. The lungs. The circulation of the blood. And it's in nature, too—day and night. Seasons, gestations." Here we go again—nature. I was waiting for that one. They can't let go of it. They talk about lungs with a cigarette in their mouths. Then they get out of breath climbing their two flights of stairs. Authentic rhythms. I don't answer. "I have nothing against modern rhythms," says Lili. "I'm not that reactionary, you know. Take jazz, for instance—syncopation is terrific. Or "Take Five," with five quarter-notes to the bar instead of four. But in your compositions, you make it impossible for people to get their bearings. We don't even know which norm we're supposed to be transgressing. That's why I call it arbitrary. Do you see what I mean?"

Of course I see what she means. She doesn't want music to take her unawares. Shake her up. Shock her. She wants to dig it right away. Come on, a bit of order in there. A bit of 1-2-3-4, if you please. Or, at the very most, 1-2-3-4-5. Let's all go marching off together. Let's all tap our feet. Let's put a bit of body back into all this. Something human. A bit of "gestation," if you please. Unthinkable for music to refer to something other than our own feeble flesh. Something other than what we already know: pee-pee, poo-poo, nite-nite. Pee-pee on time, poo-poo on time, nite-nite on time, music on time. Wake up, go to bed, eat your soup, write your symphony, get your wife pregnant. Earn your living. Life isn't free for the taking. You've got to earn it. *Earn* your life. *Kill* your time. *One*, two, three. *One*, two, three. *J*ohann Strauss. *Round* we go. *Round* we go. *Round* we go—

VARIATIO XIX: GRACE

Thomas

This ointment isn't any more effective than the last one; I'm going to have to find another dermatologist. More blank hours in a waiting-room, only to meet another hag who will conclude, just as all the others have, "My dear young man, what you have is nothing but a perfectly ordinary case of acne, a vestige of your adolescence, wash your face four times a day with Marseilles soap and you'll see, it will vanish within a week." It's been bugging me for more than six months now, whereas I never had skin problems during my adolescence. I detest pimples. Their purulence represents the eruption of the body's inside on the outside. Putrefaction on a surface that should be smooth. Madame Schneider's not much better. She urges me to find the person to whom my symptom is addressed. "Acne" sounds like "acme." "Pimple" sounds like "pimp." Perhaps I'm unconsciously resisting having to lie down on her couch and pay her, as I've been doing for the past—aha!—six months? Perhaps I'd rather be her pimp than her client? I couldn't care less, just as long as I get cured.

Pierre would make fun of that phrase, of course. He'd talk about the mind/body separation, the ultimate fraud of

Christianity. He'd call me a crypto-Catholic. According to him, psychoanalysis itself is nothing but a hyped-up version of Confession. With one major difference—it costs money. No, two: even members of the weaker sex can be initiated into the sacred mysteries of modern times. "You look a bit bewildered today—I bet you've been in a trance." He calls it a trance. This pun on the psychoanalytic concept of transference is so ridiculous that I don't even bother to answer it.

In fact our interests have done nothing but diverge for the past few years. We keep in touch because we were best friends at the age of eighteen, but basically we have to cast about for a neutral topic of conversation. He's involved in politics, he prides himself on being down-to-earth and avoiding the nihilistic opium of his contemporaries. His own opinions are always categorical, even if they vary from week to week—I find it tiring to keep up. As for me, there's no point trying to tell him how enthusiastic I've been all year about Franz Blau's seminar on "The Psychoanalysis of Opera." I know he'd just laugh. And yet that seminar's the only thing that makes my life liveable right now. Everything else bores me stiff. New books and journals keep coming out and they all sound exactly alike. Political speeches are even worse. At least Blau is exploring uncharted territory. It's quite amazing. Father, mother, son, daughter: bass, soprano, tenor, alto. So the soprano would be the mother… That really set me thinking. I once read a clinical study of a professional actress. When she was in shape, she said, her voice would become pointed, it would get bigger and bigger; sometimes it got so hard that she could almost feel it. Her whole vocabulary could have been directly transposed into sexual terms... but those of a man, not a woman. She spoke of acting as a form of "exhibitionism" and she called her voice a "tool"... I was quite impressed by this ambiguity. Returning from Blau's seminar, I put on a Callas record and tried to listen to it from this new perspective. Why had listening to great sopranos always made shivers go up and down my spine? They were shivers of fear—simultaneously voluptuous and unpleasant. Fear...that the voice might break. At the climax of an aria, just at the point that was the most beautiful and the most difficult, the voice—which had become so much more than a voice, something tangible—might waver, crack, break off and send me plummeting into the void. Like in animated cartoons where the characters don't notice they've gone two yards beyond the edge of the cliff—but as soon as they look down, the law of gravity starts functioning again. So the soprano might indeed be the mother, but not just any mother—the phallic mother? The bliss with which her voice fills us might be the bliss of incest? And the fear it arouses might be the fear of castration—a brutal encounter with the Law of the Father? I raised this question at the seminar last month, but Blau didn't look very convinced. "In that case, how would you account for the fact that for centuries men were *literally* castrated to preserve their soprano range?" At the following session, he played us an exceedingly rare recording of the only castrato to have lived in the 20th century. The audience was flabbergasted. No one had ever heard anything like it. The sonority was totally unlike that of a counter-tenor. It gave you the same sense of discomfort as when a mental retard looks you straight in the eye. His eyes are lovely, clear and trusting—and completely empty. That's what the castrato's voice was like: angelic, and therefore inhuman. Adolescent boys with exceptionally lovely voices were castrated by the Catholic church, at the age of thirteen or fourteen, so they could go on singing soprano. Women could not become members of the choir, so members of the choir became women. In fact, it was not the penis itself which was cut off, as everyone likes to imagine. A simple incision was made in each testicle to prevent the transmission of male hormones from the thyroid gland to the scrotum. Naturally, following this operation, the young men were impotent for life; they often grew monstrously fat because of the hormonal imbalance; they almost invariably died before reaching forty. For the glory of God.

But I don't see how this barbaric practise necessarily invalidates my hypothesis concerning the phallic mother. I mentioned it to Madame Schneider yesterday. She asked me to name my favourite soprano. "La Callas, of course." She replied that "Callas" could indeed be interpreted as rhyming with "phallus"—and what was more, the singer's first name, Maria, was the same as the Virgin Mother's; it thus seemed certain that I had wished to sleep with my mother. This was not exactly what I'd been attempting to clarify… But, as she has often pointed out, theoretical speculation is out of place on the couch.

I'd like to write an article about this and show it to Franz

Blau. I'd discuss Nijinski, who fell to the ground in the middle of a spectacular leap and went totally mad on the spot. They picked him up off the stage, right where he'd fallen, and shut him up in an asylum. He'd experienced the paradigmatic fall: death had erupted in the middle of life; there was no other conceivable conclusion to that particular leap. I'd also discuss the case of the young soprano who made a perfect recording of the *"Casta Diva"* and then never opened her mouth again, either to sing or speak. She had reached the acme—she knew that never again would she sing as well—so there was no point in going on. At the age of nineteen, she was as good as dead. Nineteen—that is, the same age as this young girl who came and sat down next to me. Perhaps she even looked like her. A thin, androgynous body, devoid of curves. Sopranos always gain weight on purpose, to make their diaphragms more powerful. They grow increasingly monstrous in the role of ingénues. I've seen *Traviatas* in which the Violetas looked like cows. During the final scene you would have thought they were calving, instead of fading into nothingness. Violeta should be evanescent, diaphanous, almost transparent. This girl would be admirable in the role. It's easy to imagine her wasting away with tuberculosis. Her skin becoming gradually translucent. Her limbs growing more and more fragile, their negligible weight more and more difficult to bear. The bones of her skeleton becoming visible through their envelope of flesh. Her features more and more precisely delineated, the angles of her body standing out with ever-increasing clarity. Finally, in an indiscernible instant, life would cease: her lungs would be inundated by the air for which they had been struggling a moment earlier. Her body would be nothing but pure breath.

That is the only desirable death, the only one that escapes abjection. No—there's another one, comparable in its grace: the death of the bull in a professional *feria*. *Ferias* are the only passion Pierre and I continue to share. Hélène turns up her nose and speaks of "barbaric customs." She never comes with us, thank God. But I'm sure this girl would understand the thrill of *corridas*. I'll tell Pierre about her after the concert— we'll try to imagine in detail an afternoon spent with her in Sevilla. Her name would be Ariane. She'd be sitting between the two of us. She wouldn't cry out raucously, as the Spanish women do, tossing roses and handkerchiefs into the ring. Her eyes would be glassy. She'd watch the bull and only the bull, never the matador or the picadors. She would stare as the beast executed its *danse macabre*, following every contortion and every feint. The rivulets of blood would make her shiver—not with disgust but with excitement. She'd wrap her arms around her body, her hands gripping her own ribs. We'd see her knuckles turning pink, then white. The bull would stumble, giddy with loss of blood, and she'd lean against us for support. The roars of the crowd would not even reach her ears. Beneath the glancing rays of the sun, she'd grow increasingly pale, like an overexposed photograph. And when the moment came— the sword aloft, its dazzling blade suspended, every breath withheld—her motionless body would suddenly rear up, her shoulders heave, her eyes roll back and her head loll over to await the *coup de grâce*. The blow of grace. The most graceful of all blows. To be literally struck dead by grace. Like Nijinski. Will I be able to reconstruct all this tomorrow on the couch? What hidden meaning should I be prepared to find? Ariane and the Minotaur? The labyrinth of my mother's entrails? Torero-Thorer? Mi-no-thor: I am not Thor, the god of war, Vulcan, volcano… Am I perhaps attempting to repress the Name of the Father?

VARIATIO XX: FROZEN

Anna

I should've ironed the skirt, but if I had, something else would have started to obsess me, like my badly-shaven legs or my fingernails chewed to the quick or my dirty hair. Anything, so long as it was an imperfection I could latch onto. And, as usual, I would wind up with two contradictory convictions: on the one hand, that everyone's staring at me and criticising my inappropriate behaviour and appearance, and on the other hand, that all this is pure paranoia. In fact—that is, in *actual* fact—people only ever say nice things to me. They tell me I'm beautiful, or sweet, or nice, and that I have my whole life ahead of me—how lucky I am to have so many talents and so many youthful years in which to bring them to fruition! But when my back is turned, I always have the feeling they're making fun of me, whispering things about me—things that are the truth. Like that I'm crazy. But I pretend not to hear. I always dread having to talk to people. Tonight Nathalie and I are going to leave right after the concert. We'll let her mother stay to gossip with her friends and go wait for her in the garden. Whenever I talk to people, I feel like it's some sort of game, and everyone but me is familiar with the rules. Sometimes I think I must have fallen asleep for a year or so at some point in my childhood, and it was precisely the year during which everyone else was initiated into the game. I feel totally adrift and I'm afraid people will notice, so I make a tremendous effort, I glue some expression or other onto my face in the hopes that this arrangement of my features will correspond to their idea of an "animated" or "curious" or "intelligent" young lady; I try to see myself through their eyes. But then I panic at the idea that they might actually judge me on this basis: my play-acting will inevitably lead them to form an opinion about me, an opinion which will have nothing to do with who I really am.

I'd very much like to know who I really am. I feel I could be absolutely anything but that I am in fact absolutely nothing. I pick up on whatever people project onto me, I sense the image of me they'd like the most, and try to resemble it. The worst thing is that it works. Afterwards, when I'm alone, I feel empty inside—and guilty, too, for having betrayed both the other person and myself. The whole process is so exhausting that I prefer just to be alone. Nathalie's the only person I can talk to about these things. She's exactly like me, except that she still lives with her family—she's not totally adrift. I really am alone now, most of the time. People find this very impressive. Only eighteen, and already earning your living as a model! Only eighteen, and already living in your own apartment! What a bunch of idiots. The surprising thing is not that a girl of eighteen can be independent, but that adults can't. The closer I get to adulthood, the more disappointed I

am. I'd always thought adults knew a great deal about life—
I thought they had some sort of wisdom or *savoir-faire* that I,
too, would acquire. But deep down, most of them are less
self-confident than little kids.

I find their insecurity revolting. The men who gaze into
my eyes and say, "Only eighteen years old! You're so
mature—I could have sworn you were twenty-one!"—they
disgust me. I couldn't give a shit about my age, it doesn't help
in the least, I'm just as depressed as any fifty year old, if not
more so. In fact I don't know how I'm going to make it to
fifty; it just seems impossible. I'm already so exhausted that I
have to make a superhuman effort just to get up in the morning. How does one go about *living*? How do people manage?
No one's ever explained it to me; all they say is the usual crap
about how lucky I am to be so young and so beautiful and so
on and so forth. The fantastic modeling career I have ahead
of me—and maybe an acting career, too, if some director falls
for my sexy legs. They never tell me how to surmount all the
horror and stupidity. They don't want to know about that.
What they call "stupidity" is the kids I worked with last summer, for example. That they can deal with. They're even glad
such things exist. They can put up with conspicuous madness
because they think it has nothing to do with them. When you
see swollen skulls, skinny arms, slobbery little girls who pee
their pants, bespectacled little boys who rock themselves back
and forth in a corner for hours on end, or throw a tantrum
and smash everything in sight—at least you know where you
stand. *They're* not normal, that's for sure; therefore we must

be normal. Personally, I went crazy working with them. There were twelve of them and I was in charge of the whole group every afternoon from two to seven. The only thing that interested all of them at the same time was music. All I had to do was start tapping some rhythm on a saucepan and they'd gather around me with eyes like saucers. When I sang, they were literally *enchanted*—I was like the pied piper of Hamelin. The rest of the day, time didn't go by at all; it froze. I could do a thousand things and think a thousand thoughts, and the clock would not budge. For instance, I'd be washing the sheets of an eight-year-old boy who'd shat his bed. They'd be full of crap; I'd scrub and scrub, then I'd look at how red my hands were as they twisted the heavy, water-soaked sheets, and I'd say to myself well this could just go on for ever and ever; I could be here for the rest of my *life*, in the heat of the laundry-room, clumsily twisting these sheets as droplets of sweat slid down my cheeks; it might very well *never* stop— time might just get stalled and never start up again. Filled with panic, I dropped the sheets on the floor and ran outside. One of the kids was hitting another one over the head with a big stick. The victim was weeping in silence. I grabbed the stick and started beating the aggressor, I was beside myself with rage, I screamed and screamed, I beat him for maybe a full minute—and then I saw myself from the outside, and once again I was seized at the thought that this could go on indefinitely—who was this monstrous harpy tormenting the body of a child? And I collapsed, the breath knocked out of me, amidst the crowd of crazy children.

Even Nathalie doesn't know about that.

Madness is all around us, it's right here, already inside of us, waiting until the time is ripe to rear its ugly head.

It's *horrible*.

That's what makes me so very photogenic—I have the body of a nymph and eyes that have seen *horrors*. Once in a dressing-room, I caught a glimpse of myself naked in the mirror and then stopped and stared. How could my body possibly look so fresh, when I felt so damaged inside?

I almost never look at my body, whereas it is looked at professionally from morning to night. The camera eye. The photographers who shoot me "from the right angle." I never flinch. I move when and where they tell me, in a state of total indifference. I give them nothing of myself—nothing but the surface. They'll never know my thoughts. They can't imagine how cold their compliments leave me. It's so predictable—they all say the same thing—"You look like a Botticelli painting, "The Birth of Venus." They keep trying to impress me with how cultivated they are, and that's the only painting in the world they've ever heard of. Some of them ask me to go out with them after the session; I always say no. They think it must because I'm a virgin—it's convenient for them to think I'm a virgin, whereas I was deflowered at fourteen. It turns them on to think they might be the first. Bunch of idiots. Sex doesn't interest me.

The only time I liked it was with Gabriel Elliott, who plays in Frédéric Dumont's group. I found it very flattering to be in bed with a jazz pianist. He was exactly twice my age, but that didn't matter in the least. After we'd made love, instead of wanting to split immediately the way I usually do, I felt marvellously relaxed. I said, "I love you" and he answered, "So do I." Then I said, "I want you to tell me I'm the *somethingest* mistress you've ever had." I wanted to be *very, very* something—whatever the something was. I've always been curious to know which *extreme* adjectives people would apply to me, in the hopes that this might help me define myself. With Gabriel, I finally felt enough trust to ask the question. What did he answer? "You're the *youngest* mistress I've ever had, that's for sure!"

It was like a slap in the face. I got dressed and walked out of the hotel. The dream of love was over and done with. That's what people are like—a bunch of idiots. Most of them, at least. They know nothing about either life or love, so they spend their time pretending. For example, they give chamber music concerts where they can all get together and share gossip and compare clothes. Just so they won't have to think about the horror. They know they live in a horrible world but they're incapable of changing it; all they can do is try to attenuate their leftist intellectual guilt. Nathalie and I had an idea for a film entitled *The Leftist Intellectual*. The hero is a horse. It's walking down a tree-lined country road. The weather is beautiful—a sunny spring day. The leafy branches of the trees meet overhead. Birds chirp and twitter. At the edge of the road sprout tiny soft-hued wildflowers. Looking straight ahead, the horse advances at a light, gay trot. It is wearing blinders.

It sniffs at the spring air. We see its nostrils quiver.

Then, very slowly, the camera moves away. It reveals, in the ditches along the edge of the road, rotting corpses. Children dying of hunger. Beggar women with glassy eyes and skeletal, outstretched hands. Men dangling from the branches of the trees—Black men, the victims of lynchings. Beyond them, the fields and hills are covered with the scattered limbs of dead soldiers. Still farther off, in the background, what looked like a mountain turns out to be the infinite heaps of Jews gassed at Auschwitz. Gradually, a series of moans and cries and screams of agony begin to mingle with the twittering of the birds. They grow louder and louder, reaching an intolerable level as the camera includes an ever-broader view of the horrors humanity has inflicted upon itself. Finally—all at once—the camera zooms back in on the horse. Close-up of its nostrils quivering and its ears twitching.

Here in this room, all you can hear are the twitters. No one wants to hear anything else. That's what music is for—to distract us from the horror. In the Nazi concentration camps, the prisoners themselves were forced to play in orchestras as they awaited their turn for the gas. That's exactly what I did with the crazy children—I sang to make them think about something other than their prison. And it worked, but I hated myself for it; more hateful than anything else is the fact that it works.

VARIATIO XXI: GREEN

Kenneth Kulainn

...never seen her smoke so much. She told me in the car on the way back from the station that with the world the way it is she can't trust people who don't smoke. She can't trust people who aren't neurotic. That's the way she talks now, she uses words like "neurosis," "psychosis," "paranoid," as though she were saying "tree," "flower," "house." I don't know when she started talking like that. I ache for her. Lili, my little one. My lil' Lil. Ah, Liliane, my own tiny girl. How does it come about that you have so much rage to vent? She says anger is something that helps her to live; she draws most of her strength from it. Where on earth did she learn that? Who taught her that? All through her childhood I encouraged her to discover the strengths within her and let them blossom. Her wee white body shivering with fever—I would hold her in my arms over the sink, pour lukewarm water over her burning skin, and sing to her the ballads I remembered from my own childhood—

In Dublin's fair city, where the girls are so pretty
I first set my eyes on sweet Molly Malone
As she wheeled her wheelbarrow

through streets broad and narrow
Crying "Cockles and mussels, alive-alive-oh!"...
    every verse until the last—
She died of a fever and no one could save her
And that was the end of sweet Molly Malone
Now her ghost wheels her barrow
through streets broad and narrow
Crying "Cockles and mussels, alive-alive-oh!"

Sweet Molly died of her fever, but you're still alive, Lili, I'm holding your entire life in my two hands and I'll make it into a lovely one, you'll be healthy and full of joy and light, and I went on singing—
I once was a bachelor, I lived by myself,
I worked at the weaver's trade,
And the only, only thing that I did that was wrong
Was to woo a fair young maid.
I wooed her in the wintertime
And in the summer too-oo,
And the only, only thing that I did that was wrong
Was to keep her from the foggy, foggy dew.

The two of us lived alone together, I wanted to give her everything, we kept each other warm during the long rainy winter, and every year when spring arrived I'd take her for a walk along the Aven. I'd show her the buds and newborn leaves, the miracle of nature's renewal. her eyes would open wide, she'd search the grass for the wee white flowers that grew among the blades and bring them to me. What did I do wrong?

The only, only thing that I did that was wrong
Was to keep her from the foggy, foggy dew.

The foggy, foggy dew. Next to the river. Your mother went to meet it one spring morning. You don't remember, Lili. You have memories of her but they are vague and colourless; your life in colour began that spring day of her disappearance, when I swore I'd make you shine with light and joy.

Now I see you dressed in black and it's as though Louise had come back to life. When she died she was younger than you are now. You were tiny, you don't remember, you didn't weep for her. Lil' Lil, my own wee child. I remember how gay you used to be during our holidays at the seaside, turning somersaults and cartwheels, you wanted to be an acrobat when you grew up, when did your backbone turn into an iron pole? When did you start living your life with determination instead of impishness?

She discovered the harpsichord. I'd found her a piano teacher and she seemed to be enjoying her lessons, but one day—she must have been twelve or thirteen—she discovered the harpsichord. She was morbidly attracted to that instrument. "Daddy, for Christmas, please. One wish." You were starting to grow away from me. I felt resigned—it was the onset of adolescence; I had to get used to the idea of losing you sooner or later.

She played the harpsichord from late afternoon till midnight, shut up in her room, the way she is now.

You never spoke to me anymore, you stopped showing me your poems. You became taciturn, elusive, a phantom wandering through the house. "Darling, why are you so moody these days?" "I'm moody, that's all." I tried to make light of it. "You may have a well-tempered harpsichord, but you're turning into a very bad-tempered harpsichordist." She didn't laugh. I noticed she had stopped laughing completely. But she played the harpsichord more and more.

This Bach piece—I recognize it. She's been playing it since she was sixteen. I never thought it suited her—too strict and orderly, whereas she was so graceful, so light.

Like a fairy, my wee Lil, a tiny fairy flitting among the first flowers. I'd told you about the leprechauns, those magic little men who hide in the hills of Ireland. You have to look very closely to see them because they're always dressed in green. You wanted to know if the leprechauns could see the fairies and *vice versa*. Yes of course they can, my own tiny girl. I'd dress you in green from head to foot and you'd skitter up a tree. "Can you see me, Daddy?" "No, where are you?" "I'm going to cast a spell on you." "That's impossible! I'm an ogre and I can gobble up the whole tree!" You screamed with laughter. I got down on my hands and knees at the foot of the tree. "Mmmmm, this bark is delicious, yum, yum! And, for dessert, I think I'll have a little lady leprechaun." "Don't kid yourself, Mister Ogre. I'm gonna turn you into a spider." "Aargh! Anything but that! I'll give you three wishes if you spare my life."

Three wishes. "One! I wish you'd never cry. Two! I wish

you'd always be nice to me. Three! I wish you'd sing me a lull-aby. Right now!"

We spoke together in the language of your mother, but the lullabies I sang to you were in English.

Rock-a-bye baby, on the treetop
—I can still hear your peals of laughter—
When the wind blows, the cradle will rock
When the bough breaks, the cradle will fall,
And down will come baby, cradle and all.

How does it happen that in almost every lullaby, someone dies? You'd come slithering down the tree using the swing rope and I'd go run your bath. In the evening when I tucked you into bed, you'd ask me to tell you more about the lep-rechauns. "They all know how to play the harp." "I'm going to learn how, too." Yes, Liliane, a harp would have been so much better than a harpsichord. You could have brought it with you on our morning walks along the Aven. You would have played Irish tunes on it, stroking the strings with your fingers. The harp is an instrument that allows the passage of air. There's no air whatsoever in the harpsichord. Not the least respite. Especially with Bach. The piece begins and then just keeps on going—you feel like taking a breather, stretch-ing your limbs, but it's impossible. When you took up the harpsichord, you transformed yourself from a fairy into a fury. You subjected yourself to a ferocious discipline, as if your life depended on it. You played right through the win-tertime, and through the summer, too—

But then, you did stop playing for many years.

When you left home, you didn't take your harpsichord with you. I didn't know what to do with it. There's nothing worse than a silent instrument. It's always a reproach. What were you reproaching me for? I kept trying to figure it out, but I never succeeded.

I didn't hold you back, my sweet fairy. I let you fly away. I had no choice but to trust you and hope your wings would be strong enough.

You wrote me laconic letters about your life in Paris. I was wounded by your expressions of affection at the bottom of the page. "All my hugs and kisses to my dear old Dad." I didn't know you anymore. Had I lost you, too, to the foggy, foggy dew? Your childhood seemed to have gone by in a flash. You'd disappeared into the dark. Into the fog. I heard from you less and less often. Once you showed up with your friend Pierre, without warning. We shared the meager meal I'd cooked for myself. We had nothing to say to each other. You'd wanted to show Pierre the wicker swing I'd hung from the tree—it was gone. You were furious. But why on earth would I have left it there?

Another time, you came alone at Christmas. You arrived in the middle of the night, in pouring rain, with a gift—a record of harp solos. We listened to it together, drinking the mixture of whisky and coffee that had become your favourite beverage—"Irish coffee without the sentimental cream." I noticed you drank quite a lot. Then you started asking me questions about Louise. What was she like? What did she use to talk about? What music had she loved? Why had she drowned herself? Why? And everything—the river water, the harp music, the liquid burning in our throats, Louise's impenetrable silence, the blackness of her eyes, the blackness of your eyes, the black liquid we were drinking, the black river water churning where her body had gone down—all of that flowed together and I started to cry, the tears poured from my eyes, the harp, Louise's death—ah no, ah no, Liliane—you, too, have left me alone—and you, too, started weeping and holding me in your arms and singing to me, lay thee down now and rest, may thy slumber be blest, and we fell asleep together—

Then more time went by. It does that. It brings people together who had grown apart, and then it separates them again. Now that evening is nothing but a memory for me to file away with the others—next to the laughing little girl and the sulky adolescent. The pictures hang side by side in my mind, and I can't make sense of them. I don't know you, Liliane. The woman who sent me an invitation to her performance of *The Goldberg Variations* is a perfect stranger. She has friends I've never met, problems I know nothing of, values that are foreign to me. I don't expect her to come home for a visit anymore. She hasn't come in years.

Again I'm a bachelor, I live by myself,
I work at the weaver's trade,
And the only, only thing that I do that is wrong
Is to think about my fair young maid.

I scarcely do think about her anymore. I tend to cherish my solitude now. Every morning, winter or summer, I walk alone along the Aven for hours on end. Dawn has always been my favourite time of day. In Ireland, they say it's the moment when fairy wings turn into dewdrops.

VARIATIO XXII: STRANGER

Reynaud

Maybe it's the influence of the full moon, combined with that of the summer solstice, that's giving me this feeling of pressure in my chest. Is it the atmospheric conditions, or just the atmosphere created by the concert? Perhaps it's my annual apprehensiveness at the approach of summer—I've been looking forward to this season for so long it hurts to actually enter into it, because to acknowledge that it's begun is also, inevitably, to hasten its demise. Moreover, my birthday is at the beginning of July and I'm not that keen on birthdays. Thirty-nine this year, which means I'm verging on the fateful figure of forty. When I was a kid, forty and eighty were one and the same thing. In a sense it's true, since time goes by faster and faster as you get older. My mother's nearly eighty now, and the years are nothing but a frantic race to get her ritual offerings mailed on time. Scarcely has she sent off her Christmas parcels than she has to start thinking about birthday cards for her grandchildren, and all of a sudden it's autumn again, with Christmas looming up ahead. Last month she wrote me a letter dated May 25, 1878, the body of which began, "My darling Reynaud, how time flies!" Indeed.

Thirty-nine is thrice thirteen—a lucky number multiplied by an unlucky one—I wonder what that will bring. Maybe a heart attack. I think my face is already more wrinkled than Bernald's, whereas he's got a few years on me. Wrinkles are so awfully visible on white skin—in Africa you sometimes see old men who look as if they're twenty. Blacks undergo virtually no change in appearance between forty and eighty—they slow down, that's all, and then one day they don't get up in the morning. Heart attacks are unheard-of. Once I tried to explain to them what it's like—what happens when the heart starts jumping around in the ribcage like a malicious little animal, or thumping furiously like a possessed drummer—I even showed them on the tam-tam, but they didn't really get my meaning. In their opinion, as long as I didn't provoke the acceleration myself, for example by dancing all night long at a village feast, I had nothing to fear.

I'd actually prefer to die that way—dancing to drums in Africa—rather than sitting here on my chair at a concert in Paris. Europeans have never understood the first thing about music. They have a vague idea that it has something to do with the sacred, but the idea is so diffuse, and their notion of the sacred so confused, that they wind up inventing situations of incredible discomfort. When you think about it, the conception of an evening like this one is exceedingly bizarre: thirty people from different regions, some of them even from different countries, are summoned to a particular place at a particular time. They sit down side by side facing another person, the instrumentalist. After approximately an hour and a half of relative immobility and silence, in the course of which the music is produced, they will suddenly begin to clap—all of them at once. Then they'll light up cigarettes, pour themselves alcoholic beverages, and express their opinions about what they've just heard. Each of them will congratulate the instrumentalist, either by shaking her hand or kissing her cheek. Towards midnight they'll all go home, and probably not see each other again for months or even years.

The opera is an even stranger phenomenon. People who don't know each other at all spend an entire night standing in line together at a ticket counter. This gives them the right to purchase a tiny piece of cardboard for an exorbitant sum of money. Two weeks later, they return to the same place. Now the men are wearing dark suits; long narrow ribbons, some dark and others brightly coloured, are knotted around their necks. The women have on long dresses and sparkling stones. Those who paid a little less for their cardboard have to ascend several flights of stairs, whereas the others penetrate at once into a vast, round, empty hall. The instrumentalists gradually make their appearance, only to vanish immediately into a pit. The last to arrive is a man in a special suit with two strips of material dangling below his buttocks. He has no instrument whatsoever, nothing but a short plastic or metal stick— and yet it is for him that the audience bursts into applause. The man with the stick turns around and bows from the waist. Then he climbs onto a small wooden box. He raises his stick in the air. Suddenly the hall is plunged into darkness, with the exception of an elevated platform behind the musicians, in the corner of which we can now discern a woman. She is wearing clothes that went out of style centuries ago. She crosses the platform, followed by a small circle of white light. The spectators clap even more furiously than before. The woman sings something in a language which is not that of the spectators. Meanwhile, she has been joined by a man, also decked out in clothes of another century. The woman's song draws to a close. Now it is the man's turn to sing, but he is prevented from doing so by the spectators who are shouting "Bravo! Bravo!"

That's how adults behave. Teenagers are even worse.

In a square hall, three thousand people are on their feet. The entry fee is lower than at the Opera, but that is because not a single musician is present—or even expected to be present in the course of the evening. Instead of musicians, there is a man sitting in a glass cage in the deepest recesses of the hall. On the table in front of him, two metallic disks are turning all by themselves; on each of these he sets another disk made of black plastic. Thanks to a needle oscillating in their grooves, the latter disks produce music in alternation. The music passes in turn through huge black boxes covered with holes, which amplify its volume several dozens of times. The songs played in this manner contain words—and this time the words are in the language of those who've paid to hear them—but they are made incomprehensible, firstly by the musical instruments themselves, and secondly by the volume at which they are transmitted. By contrast with the two preceding situations, the three thousand people in the room are allowed to speak, except that in order to make themselves heard they have to shout. In general, half the participants communicate in this manner, while the other half occupy the dance floor. Their dancing consists of shifting their body weight from one foot to the other to the rhythm of the music (invariable from one song to the next), while simultaneously shaking their torsos, arms, and—if room allows—hips. Each dancer shakes alone, though they usually come onto the dance floor in couples (man-woman, man-man or woman-woman). However, the dancers are so crowded together that they continually bump into one another. In addition to the brutality of the music and the dancing, this sort of place is characterized by exceedingly violent lighting effects—the dancers are constantly under fire from red, green or blue projectors—and every now and then, at irregular intervals, a white flash rips open the darkness and gives all of them a cadaverous look. Indeed, the teenagers purposely enhance this look by the way they dress, make up their faces and style their hair: whereas virtually all of them come from the city's most opulent neighbourhoods, they enjoy displaying all the external signs of the most abject poverty.

Or again—the Rolling Stones. How would one go about explaining what occurs when they perform in public? Girls weeping and moaning, boys yearning to be Mick Jagger, thousands of fans trampling each other to get closer to the stage, closer to the five fetish-bodies—and so the latter must be surrounded and protected by a dozen other muscular male bodies, or else the musicians would be attacked, their clothes and instruments damaged by the crowd; the destructive energy inherent to these performances could no longer be contained. The Who understood this very well, which is why they smashed their own equipment on stage at the end of each performance. So did Jimi Hendrix, who poured gasoline over his guitar, immolating it in front of the hysterical crowd at Woodstock. Or John Lennon…before he was shot to death by an autograph chaser.

Music has everything to do with death—we know this without really knowing it. Other cultures are far more lucid on this score. Whereas in the hypercivilised Europe of the twentieth century, music permits these mad excesses, these uncontrollable upsurgings of "savagery"—in what we call primitive societies, the connection between music and death is far better understood, and therefore better controlled as well. Among the Fataleka of Melanesia, music is used exclusively during the complex and codified performance of funeral rites. Only men have the right to play the Fataleka flutes—and only certain men. The pieces they play at each stage of the ceremony have been handed down from generation to generation "since the beginning." Not a note may be changed. The sacred sounds, and the order in which they are produced, must be perceived as totally ineluctable. Afterwards, the flutes are put away and no one may touch them. The future of the ancestor and his name depend on the rigorous respect of this law—Fataleka music is anything but a joyous daily distraction.

But what would happen if I felt the onset of a heart attack, right here and now? What would happen if my heart stopped passively following the rhythms of Bach and started beating out a piece of ragtime? What would people do? The concert would break off abruptly. Bernald would rush over: "Reynaud! Reynaud!" The women would gasp and squeal; the men would answer them in whispers. Then an ambulance would arrive, its siren howling. From the hospital, they would send a telegram to my mother. The doctors would mutter over my palpitating chest.

Everyone would move in time to my heart. They'd hook it up to a machine whose needle would faithfully reproduce its erratic pulse. My sisters would come to the concert, raising and lowering their eyebrows as the needle went up and down. Nurses would rush this way and that, banging doors behind them in the corridor. I'd try to speak. To tell them... I have the right to choose my own funeral music, that's one right accorded to dying people in this country. So listen to me—listen—I want you to play my record of tam-tam music from Black Africa. Nothing else. Will I be able to make myself clear? No requiems, no hymns, no *Eine Kleine Nachtmusik*—no, Mother, not even your precious Mozart. Nothing but tam-tams. Pure rhythm. Black hands causing the void to vibrate—that's worth so much more than all of your—

VARIATIO XXIII: JUGGLING

Student of Bernald's

"And why," my guardian angel would ask at this point, "are you always putting yourself in situations in which you feel inferior? If you'd stayed home this evening with a book, you could have listened to *The Goldberg Variations* quite painlessly. Did you really have to prove to yourself yet again that this kind of social event makes you ill at ease? How much longer are you going to run after Men Who Think, in hopes that your eyes will draw them to you like a magnet? How many more years will you go on attempting to capture intelligence with beauty?" But Bernald Thorer is different, he really is, and I can prove it—he's the one who invited me here this evening. Of all the women students who attended his seminar faithfully year after year, I'm the one he chose. He sensed that I alone understood what had happened to him—because of my letter. "Which doesn't prevent you from feeling every bit as miserable as usual." I know, but that's because I'm so overwhelmed to be here among his closest friends, to see him in a context outside of the University, especially to see his wife—she's so impressive, so statuesque…and have no way of expressing my emotion. "But don't you see—it always comes down to the same thing: it's because all this has nothing to do with your own life. Of course you're incapable of expressing what you feel, because your feelings only involve people other than yourself. We spoke of that a long time ago, in connection with movies. You let yourself get too involved in the conflicts between characters, you act as though your own interests were at stake, and in the end you're crestfallen to discover that they're not the least bit interested in you, since they vanish into thin air as soon as the lights go up. Why do you always need to live vicariously? Don't forget *Don Giovanni*—" Yes, but in that case I had no choice; it was for my thesis. I had to go and see every possible version of the opera and the play, listen to every musical rendition, read the dozens of variants of the story—and the critical analyses, at least the major ones; otherwise it wouldn't have been a serious piece of scholarship. It's true the film bowled me over completely. I thought I knew everything about the character of Don Juan, but one essential mystery remained to be solved—I'd discussed it with Thorer on two or three occasions—why *mil e tre*? It was the film that finally provided the answer. Of course, what everyone always says is that Don Juan needs a multiplicity of conquests, a really *excessive* number of them, not for the purpose of pleasure (never, in the entire course of the story, does he experience an instant of real pleasure) but in order to *write them down*, to lengthen his lista. In this sense, he is not unlike the libertines of de Sade (and "Don Juanism" is as diluted with respect to Don Juan as is "sadism" with respect to de Sade)—since in both cases the meaning of the erotic acts is coextensive with the *narrative* into which they can be transformed. The parallel, however, stops there, for Don Juan's victims are by definition consenting adults— they must be madly in love with him, and their suffering must derive exclusively from the fact that they are among the *mil e tre*—never from physical abuse.

But why does Don Giovanni love women? For he does love them—all of them—young and old, ugly and beautiful, virginal and matronly. He noses them out like an animal; he declares: "I smell woman." Women, exactly like wine (*Vivan le femmine! Viva il buon vino!*), are merely what allows him to thumb his nose at traditional morality. And this doesn't even mean Christian morality; it just means common sense, respect for others—respect for certain conventions, too, but with considerable room for *play*: infidelities, frivolities and free-for-alls—in a word, everything Don Juan abhors. Where does his categorical rejection of human values and his unshakeable loyalty to Hell come from? This remains a mystery. All we know is that he is marching firmly and resolutely towards his death.

No woman in any myth has ever achieved similar stature. No woman has ever been so convinced of the terrible inexorability of her fate. When women demonstrate comparable strength and stubbornness—Medea and Antigone are cases in point—it is always in reaction to a mortal wound inflicted on them by men. They do not inherently possess the capacity to undertake an action, for its own sake, and carry it through, whatever the cost. That's what the film shows, with pitiless clarity. However splendid they may be in their suffering,

Donna Anna and Donna Elvira are despicable for having no will of their own: not once is the initiative on their side. Anna grows proud and deceitful, Elvira oscillates between the wish to save her soul and the hope of being loved once more by Don Juan; Zerlina betrays her fiancé and, when she sees that her chances with the master are less than slim, resorts to "feminine wiles" to get him back…

Zerlina is the one who ultimately pronounces—in a parody addressed to poor, impotent Masetto—the words any woman might address to Don Giovanni: "Tear my eyes out, beat me, and I shall kiss the hand that beats me." Moaning, weeping, and hysterical, the women revolve around the man: they are prey to basely human emotions, whereas he, who provokes them, is either superhuman or inhuman. To speak his desire is the meaning of Don Juan's life; it is also what makes him superior to the women. The latter are reduced— as always, as everywhere—to answering his speech with a yes or a no.

This new idea was to form the central thrust of my thesis, and I was burning with impatience to talk it over with Bernald Thorer. If only I'd seen the film a week earlier, I would have been able to take advantage of the Master's comments on the subject. But I saw it just the night before his last lecture. I arrived late at his seminar the next day. I was in a rare state of exaltation, having spent the whole night writing down the thoughts the film had stirred in me. Everything appeared to be normal: Thorer was sitting at his table on the raised platform, surrounded as usual by a couple of dozen tape recorders, and the lecture hall was full to bursting. Naturally I had no chance of finding a seat—even the steps were clogged with students piled one on top of the other, and a fair number of them had spilled out into the corridor.

I managed to shoulder my way as far as the door, and leaned against one of the doorposts. There was no way I could get out my clipboard to take notes, so I had to content myself with listening to his voice, so melodious and familiar, choosing its words the way a child chooses pebbles on the beach.

After half an hour or so, the voice stopped. Now, there was never a "half-time break" in this seminar—besides which the idea that Thorer was developing had been left up in the air. Still, he had finished his sentence. No one could understand this totally unprecedented pause in the middle of a lecture. The students glanced at one another. Thorer hadn't left his chair, but he'd moved back in it as though to free himself of the tape recorders. Someone said, "Well?" Silence. A young woman went up to the platform to ask if Monsieur le professeur was feeling all right. Thorer simply answered, "Yes, yes." In the lecture hall, the confusion was mounting: some of the students started putting away their papers, but no one dared to just get up and leave. And then—I don't know how it happened, but as if on cue, everyone fell silent again. An absolutely delirious silence descended on the room. It lasted nearly ten minutes— Thorer staring at his students and his students staring back at him. He looked—not ill, but petrified—as though contemplating something totally unwonted. Finally, one of the cassette tapes came to an end with a

resounding click. This acted as a signal—the owners of the
tape recorders went up to the platform to reclaim them, one
by one. The other students rose and left the lecture hall in
small groups.

By the time they reached the corridor, they had already
recovered the use of their tongues. Some of them even
rewound their tapes immediately to listen to the last sentence,
convinced that, just as in sessions with their guardian angels,
the final words must have been particularly significant.

I knew this was sheer nonsense. I knew beyond the shadow of a doubt that Bernald Thorer had come to a definitive
halt after a totally arbitrary utterance. I went home. I thought
my head was going to burst. I didn't know if I felt like getting
into bed and sobbing my heart out, or shouting the good
news over the rooftops of Paris. I did neither. Instead, I made
myself a hearty breakfast—scrambled eggs, toast, honey,
orange juice and coffee. I switched on the radio; it just happened to be playing *Don Giovanni*. I switched it off and set
to eating with a fabulous appetite; looking outside, I noticed
spring had come and I wondered when.

That very evening, I sent the letter to Thorer. It contained
nothing but a quotation from Des Forêts—I'd read his novel
Le Bavard just a few days before: "Imagine a magician who,
one day, fed up with taking advantage of the gullibility of the
crowd, which he had hitherto maintained in deceitful illusion,
decides to replace the pleasure of enchantment with that of
disenchantment." That's almost an exact quote—I'd copied it
out in my notebook because I found it so delightful. Bernald

Thorer never answered my letter, of course, but I'm convinced it's the reason he invited me here tonight.

"A lot of good it does you, to know all that and still let the wool be pulled over your eyes. You're as much of a consenting victim as Don Juan's mistresses, since you want to go on being deceived. Your Jesus Christ may have turned into a Buddha, but you haven't stopped worshipping him for all that. The Holy Scriptures may have turned into a blank page, but they're still every bit as sacred to your eyes." Yes, but I have no choice. Only people with power can decide one day, with consummate majesty, to abdicate. Everyone else has to play the inglorious role of the fox eyeing the unattainable grapes. I've never been in a position of power and I've never wanted to be, so "renunciation" has no place in my vocabulary. I'm weak by nature—all I can do is absorb a bit of the strength of those around me. "There you go again, reducing yourself to naught—don't you realize how frightened you must be of your own violence, to have to keep proving how disarming you are? Being disarming is nothing but a back-handed effort to disarm others—you wish your weakness would gradually weaken everybody else. When it comes right down to it, this is why you felt so jubilant the day Bernald Thorer ceased to teach." No, no, that isn't it—

VARIATIO XXIV: SMOKE

Simon Freeson

What I wouldn't give for a cigarette—dammit, that's the hundredth time the thought has crossed my mind; it'll end up spoiling the whole concert. It's crazy. If I could just light one up, I wouldn't think about it anymore—I'd be able to concentrate fully on Bach—but it's probably no accident there are no ashtrays in sight—and I can't very well crush my cigarette butt on this waxed hardwood floor—no one else smoking?—ah yes, there's the black guy sitting next to the door—but he can toss his ashes out onto the balcony. I'd understand if there were singers or wind players—they need to breathe—but Liliane smokes herself, I saw her before the concert—so it's a perfectly arbitrary restriction. I can understand them forbidding you to smoke in libraries—wouldn't want to see the whole collection of the Bibliothèque Nationale go up in flames just because of a negligent dissertation student—although I've been in libraries where smoking was allowed—that was fantastic—it was like reading in your own armchair at home—couldn't ask for more. If smoking was allowed at the Nationale, I'd set up a cot in the main reading-room—right next to Diderot and d'Alembert's *Encyclopedia*—I'd never leave except to take a leak. As it is, I have to get up at least once an hour, it's really a drag—I do my best to get through a hundred pages before I go out to the courtyard—sometimes it isn't easy, because of the very contents of what I'm reading. You know what I mean, don't you, Bernald? Nobody makes me want to chain-smoke like Giordano Bruno, for instance. When I read him at home, I get all excited—I take notes and light one cigarette after another—once I got so carried away I almost lit my pen and wrote with my cigarette. I told Bernald about it—we'd gone for a drink together after closing time—but he didn't seem to understand at the time. Now he would. Maybe he should have taken up smoking himself.

What a scene! Never would I have expected that of him. I'd been seeing him at the BN for maybe fifteen years—we weren't buddies or anything, but we'd chat from time to time—we'd watched each other ageing among our piles of books—he didn't come as regularly as I did, more in phases—but he'd always ask for a seat close to the exit, just like me—I don't know why, since he wasn't constantly going out for a smoke. He was a far more distinguished user than I was—dissertation students would point him out to each other and whisper his name. "That's Thorer." "Are you sure?" "Sure I'm sure!" "But he looks so young! I thought he was at least eighty!"—and so forth. Personally, I wouldn't like to be recognized at the BN—I need to work in a neutral atmosphere, incognito, as it were. Fortunately, scientists are rarely rocketed to superstar status like ideologists—people know their names but not their faces—which is fine with me. Bernald, nothing doing—if he wanted to get any work done, he had to ignore the commotion produced by his presence—and I must say he was pretty good at it. He'd build himself a sort of fortress with his books—hide behind them and not emerge until eight o'clock. I'd teased him about this—told him he was going to turn into one of those doddery old men we saw all the time— bent over at ninety degrees from the waist from having spent sixty years with their noses in books—they were incapable of straightening up—like they wanted to have their bow ready for the day they entered the Académie française. Bernald laughed—he enjoyed my sense of humour. We'd chew the rag fairly often—he'd ask me about my work—and not just for the sake of conversation—sometimes he'd find analogies between his research and my own—we never talked for very long—never even exchanged phone numbers—but there was a sense of rapport. I just liked the guy. Not that this made me particularly original—everybody liked the guy. He'd always say good morning to the employees—even the coat-check lady—he'd gossip a few minutes with the curator—and I had the impression his books arrived faster than other people's, but I could be wrong about that. In any case he was well-liked— which is why people took it so badly the day he flipped his lid. If it had been some anonymous reader, they would just have kicked him out and left it at that. But you can't treat Bernald Thorer like a bum off the street.

I smelled something fishy almost immediately—that day I was practically right next to him, three or four rows closer to the door. Around ten in the morning—just when everyone had gotten settled in and the bustle of the first hour had calmed down—I heard this chuckle. I looked up—Bernald was laughing. I found this sort of rude—but then it stopped; he fell silent, I went back to my book. Maybe ten minutes later, he started laughing again—and this time it wasn't a chuckle—more like a belly-laugh; a real, honest-to-goodness guffaw. Everybody turned around to see what was going on—fortunately, it broke off almost immediately. The attendants looked a bit worried—I could see them discussing the incident in low voices—"Was that Bernald Thorer?" "Yes, it was." "But that's impossible, you must be mistaken." Personally, I was feeling a bit uncomfortable—I mean OK, he could've been reading something funny—but I couldn't see why he had to laugh *that* loud—wasn't like him, there was something fishy about it. Anyway, not another peep out of him for the rest of the morning. We went out for a sandwich together at noon. I asked him what he was reading and he answered Herodotus. At first I was a bit nonplussed—I'd never thought of Herodotus as being particularly hysterical—but Bernald told me about one or two passages and they really were hilarious—especially since he knew how to tell a story—by the time he'd finished we were both shaking with laughter. Still, it wasn't the same thing in a coffee-shop as in the BN. But I did feel somewhat reassured—Bernald acted anything but nuts—he'd put me in such a good mood that I even paid for his sandwich and glass of wine.

After lunch, I always feel a bit drowsy—I like to leaf

through scientific journals while I'm digesting my meal—
that day the library was more crowded than usual, a bit hot
and stuffy. Around three o'clock I went back to work—I'd all
but forgotten about the morning's incident—when suddenly
I heard this strangled sob. Oh, no, you're kidding, I said to
myself—he's not going to start blubbering, is he? More
Herodotus? It made me nervous—I didn't like this one bit—
and I went out for a smoke. When I got back I could hear
Bernald all the way from the door—he was crying like a
baby—I felt embarrassed for him. There was a small crowd of
people around him—other readers, attendants—the poor
guys were totally at a loss. They didn't know what to do.
Bernald was shaken by these great, wracking sobs—I came
closer and saw he had his head on his arms, his shoulders
were heaving—it was as if he'd just lost his best friend. People
were saying "Monsieur Thorer, is there anything we can do
for you?"—"Monsieur Thorer, don't you want to step outside
for a moment?"—"Please, Monsieur Thorer."

What the hell he'd read to put him in a state like that, I
haven't the slightest—probably some atrocities that took
place twenty-five centuries ago—I thought he was going too
far. I went over and took him by the arm—he put up no
resistance—I led him outside—half the reading-room was on
its feet—young bespectacled females followed us out into the
courtyard—I motioned them to keep away. Bernald stopped
crying once we got outside—his eyes were all red and puffy.
I didn't know what to say. "Do you want me to go get your
briefcase?" He nodded—I brought his things and he left

without saying good-bye—walking very slowly. Looking like an old, old man. It shook me up so badly I couldn't work anymore that day. I went home too.

Bernald never set foot in the BN again. I didn't dare try to get in touch with him—we'd never exchanged phone numbers—but I'd hear the rumours going around about him and I just couldn't fit it all together in my head. A few months later, they started reprinting his early books—the newspapers talked about him as if he were dead—I found that shocking, but there was nothing I could do.

He doesn't look dead at all—as a matter of fact he looks in better shape than ever. And if he's found himself a beautiful and cultivated wife, so much the better. I'd rather see him laughing and crying because of her than because of Herodotus. I'd give up my own research under those conditions, if I could get by with resting on my laurels—who wouldn't? Well, Dad wouldn't, of course—him and his philosophy—his love of wisdom, as he called it. It's true he was in love with it—he used to take those big, fat volumes to bed with him—Mom had to drag them out when she made the bed the next morning—that's what I call a real philosopher. I myself don't keep a single book in the bedroom—nothing but the bed and an ashtray. I thought it was disgusting, the way Dad used to read all the time—in bed, at the dinner table, in the can for hours on end—whenever I wanted to ask him something, there'd always be a book between his face and mine—it was infuriating. And where did it get him? Now my own books are selling well—it makes him gnash his teeth to see that physics can be just as popular as metaphysics—but I don't give a hoot in hell. He always gets in a dig at me when I go home for a visit—he's a tiny wizened old man now, whereas he seemed colossal when I was a kid—tells me I'd do better using my genius to find a cure for cancer—with the three packs I put away a day. He's right—I do smoke too much—I'll never live to be as old as him—maybe it's a good thing, too, judging from what a pitiful spectacle he makes—what good did his love of wisdom do him, now that he has to piss in a plastic bag attached to his belly? And with Mom out of the picture, nobody there to take his books out of the bed, he's liable to be found one of these days smothered beneath the complete works of Aristotle. Oh, for Christ's sake—I'd give anything for a smoke—how much longer is this thing going to last?

VARIATIO XXV: CUT OFF

Viviane

This is the most melancholic of all the variations in a minor key. Its slowness almost makes you lose the continuity of the melodic line; you could follow nothing but the harmony as it wends its way through shady groves: Lethe, the river of oblivion. You could close your eyes and forget about all the rest. Lethe, Liliane, I wish I could forget that you are here, not have to look at your body and its exhibition, not have to wonder what the others are thinking as they watch you. Witnessing the physical production of music has always seemed incongruous to me; I don't like being near violinists dripping with sweat, saxophonists with puffed-out cheeks, trumpetists whose eyes pop out of their sockets; I don't like to see the saliva dripping from the bottom of an oboe; I wish it were possible to forget the effort of the bodies which are coupling with the instruments for my pleasure. You, Liliane—you're like those stone flutes in the desert: the wind blows through them, but they are never touched by human hands. The genius of men moves through you and you remain impassive; no one has a hold on you—I'm glad of that, at least. It's hard for me in general, these days—I told you this on the phone this afternoon—to go out in public. I tend more and more to stay cooped up at home. Our society seems to me so very sick that I sometimes think I'm the one who must be sick. When I go to a symphony orchestra concert, I see the conductor who is a man, the musicians who are virtually all men, I look at the program and all the composers are men; during the intermission I listen to the men talking to one another; they say: "Allow me to introduce my wife" and then carry on in their booming voices, while the wives stand glued to their sides like so many umbrellas. It depresses me so much that I can't listen to the symphony. I try to cheer myself up by going to the movies. I choose a Marx Brothers film and by the end of it I'm in tears: the wild antics of four men, the incomparable joys of male bonding, the misogynous jokes that still make the audience roar with laughter. Everyone finds them funny, including the women: I think there's nothing sadder in the world than a woman laughing at another woman's expense.

I've always mistrusted roars of laughter, and every other kind of mass enthusiasm: the militant May Day demonstrations remind me of military marches, I can't see how they're any different. In both cases it's men marching together, shouting the slogans they've been told to shout, singing at the tops of their lungs for the millionth time that this is the final struggle. It also reminds me of the Catholic congregations of my childhood, singing at the tops of their lungs for the millionth time that the Saviour was born—except that hymns and carols are far more beautiful than the *Internationale*. But the illusion is the same: we're all nice and cuddly cozy together lined up in rows, and the leader, be he politician or priest, will tell us what to do, what to think and who our main enemy is. Liliane, did you know that orthodox Muslims were against every form of music—even military marches—on the pretext that music is licentious and might engender immoral conduct? That's ridiculous, I know, but before people catch onto the resemblance between military marches and the violent aspects of male sexuality, we're liable to be in for several more centuries of massacre and rape. The two are so inextricably linked in my mind that just thinking about it gives me goose-pimples. Contemporary music—I mean the music of today's youth—produces exactly the same effect on me as *Deutschland Über Alles*. Speaking of which, I don't see anything funny about punks wearing swastikas. Ostensibly, their intention is ironic. The only problem is that they really do have fascistic tendencies—inside as well as out. Once I saw this punk couple, the girl had a chain around her neck and she was literally being dragged on a leash by her boyfriend. They probably thought it was a provocative little joke, but it made me nauseous. Just as it makes me nauseous to listen to the phallic rhythms of their music—I know, Liliane, you'll say I take things too seriously, and that the choice a name like "Sex Pistols" is ironic, too—but I insist: it's serious, and all the more serious since this equivalence between the penis and a deadly weapon is so deeply imprinted in our minds as to be taken for granted.

I used to go out with a rock musician—yes, you may be

surprised, but I did have male friends at one time—during the unisex utopia of the sixties, long before I met you, when it was still bearable for me to talk with men—his name was Michel and he was an excellent musician. He played lead guitar in a group that had achieved some notoriety; he'd become the main attraction. He always smoked hash before the beginning of a performance, and on stage he'd go soaring—like a shooting star was the way he put it. In the middle of a piece he'd take off on a fantastic solo, the whole audience would hold its breath and Michel would take them soaring with them on his flying carpet. Once I told him I envied him his ability to let go so completely, to express himself through music with such absolute abandon. And do you know what he answered? When he'd smoked, and found himself under the spotlight in front of a crowd, he felt omnipotent, like a god. His body mingled with the light and his guitar became a gorgeous, throbbing erection, and when he threw his hips forward as the sound came out, it was as if he were showering the whole audience with his sperm. The music was an inexhaustible jet of sperm shooting from his body through the instrument; at such times he was literally out of this world.

I said to myself, if that's what it means to men, what about women? I went around putting this question to various people I met: what does it mean for a woman to make music? They thought I'd gone batty. A woman who makes music is like a man who makes music, only she's a woman. Oh. What about you, Liliane? Tonight you're playing a piece composed by a man, paid for by a church or a monarchy entirely structured by men, on an instrument manufactured by a man—but the fact that you're a woman is totally irrelevant?

You never wanted to believe that story I told you—but I can't help it, it's true: a sculpture exhibit in Paris had to be cancelled because it turned out that one of the statues, ostensibly representing the torso of a woman, had been fashioned with the real torso of a real woman. Given that, what does it mean for a woman to be a sculptor?

You see, Liliane, I'm a hopeless case. Once you've started seeing reality this way, it's hard to stop. And it's even worse than that—you can't imagine how far my obsession goes. I sit here watching you and it makes me sad, because I see you're still in the seduction game up to your neck—literally, up to the string of pearls around your neck—it saddens me because I keep thinking that together we might have been strong enough to invent something different. But you need a man at your side; you need his approval and his love (I don't question his love for you—that isn't the point); and you willingly don the disguise of decadence and self-irony. I'm not much better—you, at least, need something, whereas I can't even manage that; I feel defeated.

The endless martyrdom of women used to incite me to vociferate; now it leaves me increasingly voiceless. I hear choruses proclaiming that, in the final analysis, women have been happier than men. They haven't had to work as hard or go through military service. Separate, separate—above all, never attempt to think about sex and war at *the same time*. Unless it's to say that in our day and age, women can finally become soldiers. Unless it's to create a punk rock group called the Sex Pistols. Above all, never suggest that men's warmaking might have something to do with their sex. And yet… in all places, Liliane, and at all times—I know you hate sentences that begin that way, but I'll continue since you can't hear me—in all places and at all times, it has been deemed necessary to inscribe women's weakness on their bodies. I'm sure that in the "Women's Studies" departments of American universities, a number of doctoral dissertations have already been devoted to foot-binding in China or corsets in France. I came across yet another example the other day—I don't know why I continue to read, what I read only makes me want to crawl deeper into my hole—in an article about a primitive tribe somewhere in the Pacific Isles. During funerary rites, a sacrifice is demanded of each member of the family of the deceased, to accompany his soul to the nether world, and these sacrifices are differentiated according to sex. (The rite as a whole was conceived by men and concerns only male corpses, since women never become ancestors—but that, being self-evident, was not even mentioned in the article.) The little boys give a chicken or a pig. The little girls give…a finger. Every time an uncle, a brother or a cousin dies, their female relatives have one finger cut off. The adult women of the tribe are left with four or five fingers in all—the thumbs are always preserved, along with two or three fingers of the right hand, so that they may continue weaving baskets—a quintessentially female talent, as you know.

So I read that, and suddenly I had this vision of your hands, your long, delicate fingers I've kissed so often. I started calling your name, louder and louder, and—would you believe it, Liliane? —I went and locked myself up in the closet like a little girl. My whole body was trembling; I never wanted to come out again.

I'm so afraid of everything now. I'm afraid of turning into an old maid who doesn't dare go out at all, who stays at home with her cats and her tinned food. I'm afraid to read, I'm afraid to listen to people talking, I'm afraid of their cynicism and their contempt.

I sit here watching your hands on the keyboard, and instead of rejoicing, I think of the mutilated hands of those little girls. It isn't natural—I know this is what's called an *idée fixe* in psychological jargon. So help me to forget, Liliane— you're the only one who's ever been able to calm my fears. When we'd walk down the street together with our arms around each other's waists, lilting and in love—do you remember?—we weren't afraid of anything. When we'd wake up together in the morning, all we needed to do was laugh and our nightmares would dissolve into thin air. Why have I wound up so alone? And why am I alone unable to forget?

VARIATIO XXVI: FALSE

Claude

Splendid, just splendid! The way the left hand leaps across and falls exactly on the right chord, while the right hand goes on tickling the bass notes. Bravo! When it's over I'm going to jump to my feet and shout, "Bravo!" She sure will have given us one hell of a show this evening, if I may express my humble opinion. Tickled all the strings of our souls, one after the other. We will have experienced something together—even if we've never met before, we'll feel as if we all knew each other. The music will have broken the ice, and we can go directly from there to raising our glasses in a toast: "To the artist!" It really is quite amazing—music, the universal language. Little does it matter that we come from different social classes or hold different political opinions; music brings us together instantly—because emotions are the same for the entire human race.

In the car, that Bach *Partita* for solo violin, played by Oistrakh, I cried and cried and cried just listening—that was perfection incarnate, every aspiration of humanity, every noble movement of the spirit, but then I said to myself, "*Why* are you crying? For whose benefit? Now that nobody's watching and you don't have to pretend anymore." What do you mean, pretend? I'm crying because it's so beautiful! "What makes you think it's beautiful? You just think it must be beautiful because you know the names of Bach and Oistrakh!" What are you talking about? It's beautiful, that's all there is to it, and I have the right to cry if I feel like it. Jesus Christ. Reminds me of when I was seventeen, and I started drinking with my friends; my parents were firmly against it but for me it was a challenge to be able to hold my liquor. I'd put away half a dozen beers or four scotches in the course of an evening. It would loosen my tongue, I'd be the centre of attention, I'd make everybody laugh... And then one day, when my parents were out, I poured myself a glass of scotch and downed it in one gulp: "What the hell are you drinking for?" I'm drinking because I enjoy drinking! "What makes you think you enjoy it? There's no one around to impress, so what's the point of drinking?" I'm drinking because it tastes good, dammit! "Two years ago, you thought it tasted disgusting." And so forth. "Maybe you enjoy the taste because you know it's forbidden? And what's more—stolen?" Shi-it. That's what they call the voice of conscience? I call it a bunch of shit. Drives me nuts. Never leaves me alone. "Why are you going to shout bravo when it's over? Why are you going to propose a toast to the artist?" Bugger off.

The more I try to prove I can want something on my own, the more I feel the need to drink when no one's around, and the more pitilessly I am tortured by the accusations of lying.

I can't drown them out; they just keep getting louder and louder. "Help!" Die!

The worst is when I'm with other people. A friend is telling me about her problems with her boyfriend. I listen, nodding my head and squeezing her hand. She looks at me gratefully. And then I hear: "What a hypocrite! You haven't heard half of what she's been saying. You've been thinking about how you'll have to go down and buy some scotch before the stores close." I try to talk louder than the voice nagging inside my head. "Do tell me if there's anything I can do to help—and please don't hesitate to call me." "Come off it! You hate being interrupted by the phone when you're working. That is, when you're pretending to work." What do you mean, pretending? I'm doing a real translation of a real book, if you don't mind. For a real publishing house, what's more, and with a real contract. Where do you see the pretending in that? Then there's this gale of laughter in my head. I throw another scotch in just to add to the confusion.

Even when I buy a bottle, I always think they're going to ask me if I have my parents' permission. Every time I have a drink at a cocktail party—like the one there's going to be after the concert—I expect to feel a heavy hand drop onto my shoulder: "What do you think you're doing?" But it's just orange juice! Besides, I have the right to drink now! I'm thirty-five years old! So maybe there is a drop of scotch in it—okay, so what? Sometimes it's other people who make me jumpy. "How did you find the concert?" I've got my answer all prepared: It was absolutely divine, and so on and so forth. Then they'll say, for example, "In my opinion, it was utterly spoiled by the acoustics. Imagine giving a concert in a room with such high ceilings! And leaving the balcony doors open so we could hear all the noises from the street!" Yes, yes, of course, that's true, they should have been closed. Then I hear people behind me muttering to each other, "Claude isn't particularly brilliant, is he?" Can they really have said that? They can't have—cultivated people don't talk that way. Then Madame Kulainn will say: "Who took the glass I set down here a second ago?" It must be me, I'm sorry. I'm dreadfully sorry, I don't know what I was thinking. "But Claude, it wasn't you—you're drinking scotch and mine was bourbon!" Oh yes, excuse me, I did help myself to a bit of scotch, thank you so very much. "Help yourself to as much as you want, Claude, that's what it's there for!" As much as I want… "How much do you think you'll be wanting tonight? Half a bottle? A whole one? Two?"

Or else I'll say something like: it really is quite amazing—music, the universal language… And someone will pounce on me: "As usual, Claude, you only open your mouth to change feet. At the moment I happen to be preparing a series of articles on the subject of universal languages, and I can assure you that music is anything but that. Seriously, what do we grasp of the music played in Timbuktu? Or in Tibet? What makes you think the Australian aborigines would be any more capable of grasping *The Goldberg Variations*?" Naturally, naturally. That wasn't what I meant. "Why did you say it, then? Why do you just blurt out the first thing that comes into your head?"

I'll hear someone whisper, "Don't be too hard on Claude, he's completely drunk tonight." What do you mean, I'm drunk? What do you mean, don't be too hard on me? Stop treating me like a kid; I'm thirty-five years old! "Thirty-six, Claude." Not yet! "Come on, now, you're thirty-six—that's no reason to drink yourself blind." Sometimes I lie for no reason at all. "Claude—did you taste these cashews?" No… whereas I've already had five fistfuls of them. "Have some, have some, go ahead." Thanks so much—they look delicious. Or someone will say, "Have you seen Fellini's latest film?" Yes. The word is out of my mouth before I have time to think. "What did you think of the scene where…?" Very interesting, very interesting. Why do I put myself into such predicaments? "You see, dear? Claude found that scene very interesting. You're the only one who didn't." Then the husband lumbers over: "Come off it, Claude. I can't believe such a thing of you. What on earth can you have found interesting about it?"

Maybe I could sneak out before the end of the concert.

"Why did you vanish like that, Claude? We felt rather hurt." My mother is ill. "But I spoke to her on the phone at noon—she said she'd never felt better!" Yeah, but she got a bad stomach-ache towards evening. "Why did you tell Madame Kulainn I had a stomach-ache?" Er, well, I had this sort of flash during the concert—I saw you ill in bed. "Wishful thinking, maybe?" Oh, Mother.

"Claude! Are you the one who's been rummaging around in my drawers? All the letters and photographs are topsy-turvy! What in heaven's name were you looking for?" I was looking for some paper. "You know very well I don't keep paper in my bedroom! If you want some paper, all you have to do is ask for it!" Yes, Mother.

"Claude! Are you the one who's been eating the chocolate I bought for your birthday cake?…That's just too bad, then—no cake for you."

"Claude! How many hours have you spent in front of the TV set today?" Just two. "He's lying, Daddy—it's been at least four hours—I counted!" "Your sister says four hours, Claude. When are you going to learn to tell the truth?"

"Claude! Are you the one who tore your little sister's notebook? No supper for you tonight!"

Every time I walk into a restaurant: "Who gave you permission?" I don't need anyone's permission anymore; I earn my own living, I'm thirty-six years old, I can do whatever I want.

Every time I cross a border: "What are you going to tell them about your nationality? And your job? And how long you plan to stay? And the contents of your suitcase?" What do you mean, what am I going to tell them? The truth, of course. I'm not guilty! My papers are in order, I haven't done anything wrong. When I actually get searched at customs, when they go through my suitcases, it makes me feel terrific. The more painstakingly they search, the better I feel. If they find nothing, that will prove I'm not guilty. They go through the names in my address book, they compare my face, feature by feature, with the photo in my passport… I feel like saying: Go ahead, go ahead, I'm at your disposal! And when they finally let me through, I could jump for joy. Now there's no doubt about it.

They found nothing. "Well, you were lucky this time. Just wait and see what's in store for you on the way back." But for the time being, tra-la-la, I'm free! I have nothing on my conscience, nya-nya-nya. I feel all gay and frisky, just like the hands of the artist as they leap into the air and gracefully alight. It's really quite amazing the way she manages those cross-arm stunts—at lightning speed, too. Hands soaring and plunging like birds of prey. Don't you agree? Or is that just another commonplace? One thing's for sure, anyway— Madame Kulainn is one hell of an artist. Or maybe it's Bach.

VARIATIO XXVII: MEASURE

Nathalie Fournier

I can't, I can't, I just can't remember. Were there thirty or thirty-one of them? I checked it just yesterday on Mother's copy
of the music; I thought okay, it's like the days of the month,
but did I mean months with 30 days or months with 31 days?
If there were 31 variations that would make 33 pieces in all,
including the repetition of the aria, and that's unlikely since I
would have remembered 33, it's one of my favourite numbers,
it contains two 3's and it's also the product of 3 and 11, 11 is nice
because it's a prime number; the nice numbers are 1, 3, 7, 11,
13, 17, 19—I myself turned 18 this year and that's why I've fall-
en ill, as they put it, but as soon as my 19th birthday comes
round I'll get better, they'll see, especially since it falls on a
Sunday this year and that's another good sign, the first day of
the week, you can get off on a new foot, some people claim
Monday is the first day of the week but they're wrong—it'll be
Sunday the 1st of December, the first day of my 19th year, actually my 20th year but the first day of being 19. 20 is awful. I
don't even want to think about it, I don't know how any girl
can stand reaching the age of 20. They must feel so ashamed.
From then on you start counting backwards, as Mother says,

thinking she's funny. But how many variations are there? I know it was like the days of a month but even the months aren't accurate, they need to be constantly readjusted, every 4 years you have to add 1 day to the month of February, every century you have to refrain from adding it, and so on and so forth, it's because the moon and the sun won't have anything to do with one another, people try to coordinate them, they say the moon is a month and the sun is a year so there are 12 moons in 1 sun, that horrible number 12 which allows itself to be divided by practically anything, 2, 3, 4, 6, but in fact their system doesn't work, the moon and the sun can't stand the sight of each other. So then they try to convince you that women and the moon are in sync—that's even better, women have a 28-day cycle. Okay, it's not exactly 1 month but it still gets called the menstrual cycle, which is the same thing as mensual, and we get told it's connected to the phases of the moon and everybody makes as if this was all very precise and scientific, as clear as day, whereas in fact nothing could be more fuzzy and unpredictable. That must be why my periods have stopped, just to show them I wasn't just a tidal wave which could be shoved around this way and that by the forces of nature, I can control my own body, thank you very much, I can decide all by myself whether I want to bleed or not. The doctors say it's because I haven't been eating enough, they say you have to maintain a certain minimal body weight or you stop menstruating. That's a lie. My appetite's just fine. I eat exactly what I want. Everybody tries to force me to eat more: don't you want some spaghetti, darling? You used to love it! I hate your bloody spaghetti. I can't stand all those pale, insipid foods—rice, mashed potatoes, noodles—they make me almost dizzy with disgust. It's as if they were going to swallow me, instead of the other way around. I've told you 1000 times, Mother, I can look after my own meals. You don't need to make any culinary efforts on my behalf, I assure you that after half an apple and a slice of cheese I'm not hungry anymore, you have to let me decide for myself from now on. I wouldn't mind a bit of lettuce—and then she whops a gigantic heap of salad onto my plate and I get mad. I said a bit! I just wanted 2 leaves! But darling, salad isn't fattening! I bet you anything she puts extra oil in the dressing on purpose, maybe even hides some fried bacon and bread crumbs underneath, so I don't even touch it. It's not a question of gaining weight, it's just that I have to be able to count what I eat, and she can't expect me to count every single grain of rice, that would be ludicrous. She's always after me with her Darling. Father's different, he says: let her sit there till her plate's empty, so I stay at the dinner table until 10 o'clock at night and contemplate the mountain of cold, clammy mashed potatoes, thinking about nothing, waiting for them to tell me to go up to bed. Mother comes in to kiss me goodnight. She tells me Father only means well, it's because he's worried about my health. I say stop treating me like a little girl. Both of you are just the same, you want to decide everything for me. I tell you I want to take singing lessons, you tell me to do this or that instead. We know what's best, we have more experience than you. I've had it up to here. The last thing I want is to benefit from your experience and end up as dumb as you. Can't you just leave me alone? When I'm alone at last and lying awake in bed, I think about limits, that's my favourite subject. I wonder if there's an exact borderline between waking and sleeping, speaking and singing, youth and old age, thinness and obesity, I think about the paradox our Philosophy teacher explained to us, how it's impossible to cross a room because first you cover half the distance, then half of the remaining half, and so on and so forth. Theoretically, you can never reach the door, I just love that. Last night I got thinking about babies, wondering when they become human beings. Is it a murder if you perform a late abortion at the same stage as a premature delivery, and when is the precise moment of a baby's birth, when its head emerges from the vagina or its whole body or when the umbilical cord is cut? And then during the night I had this dream where two gazelles were fighting, a male and a female, and the female died. She was bathing in her own milk and blood, but the male was still alive and I had to feed it, so I did this by pouring raisins, nuts and grains directly into its gullet because its throat had been torn open, it was just about dying, too. The whole thing was horrible, all because my throat was sore from having sung so hard the whole day. I think I already sing as well as some professional sopranos, not the most famous ones of course, but with proper training my voice could be fabulous. The great French soprano Nathalie Fournier, a single performance at Carnegie Hall, with excerpts from operas by Verdi, Puccini, Bellini, as well as a few ballads by Debussy. A really quite extraordinary young singer, have you heard her? No, but I've read the rave reviews in the papers. She's only 19 years old! It's quite uncanny, her voice is so mature. In addition to which she's perfectly lovely, she looks like a swan. And that voice! As hypnotic as siren song—

Nathalie Fournier agreed to give us an interview, despite the fact that generally speaking she shies away from journalists. She received us early in the morning in her hotel room and served us breakfast on the balcony, which looked out over Central Park. She herself had nothing but black coffee.

"Don't you ever have breakfast, Mademoiselle Fournier?"

"Never. No lunch either."

"How do you manage to have such a powerful voice?"

"The voice of a true singer, Monsieur, comes from her soul. It has nothing to do with the body."

Bravo! Bravo! Nathalie Fournier, the sensation of the season, was given 3 successive ovations at Carnegie Hall. She modestly accepted a bouquet of white roses presented to her by the Mayor of New York City in person.

"We hope you intend to return to our little town, which will always welcome you with open arms."

"Thank you very much, Monsieur. Will you be joining us for champagne after the concert?"

I shouldn't have had that glass of champagne before the concert. I can feel it backing up into my throat. It's because Monsieur Thorer offered it to me and I find him so attractive I simply couldn't refuse. We clinked glasses and he looked deep into my eyes. He even told me I was wearing a lovely dress tonight, though of course the only other woman in the room at that point was the fat slob who's now sitting in the front row; next to her, even Mother would look pretty. I saw her walk straight over to the balcony and cut herself a giant slice of cake with this sort of phony nonchalance. I knew very well she felt despicable for doing that and she'd probably had to summon up all her courage to cross the room with a look on her face that said, after all I'm hungry and the cake was put here for the guests, what's the difference if I eat it now or later. I'd never never never do a thing like that, especially right in front of the host. I can control myself. He told me I was a bit pale and I said it was because I'd slept badly these past few days. He said he often had difficulty sleeping as well. I think he wouldn't have admitted this to just anybody. I bet he doesn't even sleep with his wife. She's too old, and even if she does look thin she might have fat thighs. You can't tell with those old-fashioned dresses she wears all the time. Anyway, I don't find her beautiful, a lot less beautiful than Anna, for example. Anna's by far the most beautiful woman in this room. When I ask her how she manages to stay so thin given that she eats 10 times as much as I do, she says it's because she's constantly thinking about other people's hunger and that burns off calories, whereas all I have to do is eat a whole apple instead of half an apple, that is, 70 calories instead of 35, and right away I can feel my stomach swelling, I can barely zip up my pants. But at least now I know myself, and sometimes in the middle of the night I get out of bed—

She descends the staircase noiselessly, like Lady Macbeth in her white lace nightgown. She floats into the kitchen and opens a packet of cookies, preferably the Russian cigar cookies people serve with champagne. She counts them. There are 8 per row and 3 rows in all. She mustn't eat all of them because that would make 24, a number so divisible as to be truly terrifying, so maybe she could stop at 7, only that would leave 1 in the first row, so maybe 13 but that would be too close to exactly half, so she goes on eating, chewing slowly and without hunger, counting and wondering when would be the best time to stop. For example, she could stop when she reaches 17, since during the afternoon she had eaten 17 cherries and the second transgression would cancel out the first; in the end she decides to eat them all so she can throw away the empty packet and her parents won't suspect anything. Afterwards she rushes to the bathroom and leans over the sink; the sink is better than the toilet because you can avoid the noise of flushing. Usually she doesn't even need to stick her fingers down her throat; it comes back up by itself, the way the champagne is coming up my gullet now, the way the blood will start gurgling in my vagina again one of these days, bubbling out and streaming down my thighs: when I'm good and ready.

VARIATIO XXVIII: FATIGUE

Manuel

...the mind wanders and finds nothing to latch onto. Reality stands before it like a smooth white wall. One's mental faculties coagulate, one's limbs go numb, boredom grows heavy and palpable. On the wall of reality, a single word is scrawled over and over: *anachronism*. The constraint of silence crushes everyone in its talons. Thinking beings are compelled to remain silent and to wait for the trial to end.

Bibi, I'll forgive you everything but please, in future, spare me this. My rational self is swayed by your arguments but my physical self refuses to be convinced. The repressed yawn spreads throughout my body: whenever I subject myself to the code of good manners my heart slows down, my lungs start to wilt, and my cock—miffed at being squashed between politely-crossed thighs—falls asleep and refuses to wake up for the rest of the evening. Despite all your objections, I continue to think that classical music is profoundly anti-sexual, and therefore anti-social. I know it irritates you when I express this idea in the form of a slogan: classical music is class music. But how can you deny that it was conceived, not to *épater les bourgeois*, but to put them to sleep?

And sleep is Enemy Number 1. You also object when I drink coffee at night, so as to be able to read before I go to bed. But one absolutely must remain vigilant—and only at night do I have time for reading. After dinner, when I take the Italian coffeepot full of that thick, dark brew, and settle down at the table to renew contact with Gramsci, or Benjamin, or Adorno, it's as if I were really talking to them in a café somewhere. I see the lights go out one by one in the apartment building across the street; I sense that before long, mine will be the only lamp still burning, and that it's important for me to stay awake. On pain of being engulfed by the shadows of ignorance. Long live the Enlightenment! —Can you imagine adepts of J.S. Bach helping to foment the French Revolution?

Bibi, aren't you aware of the aristocratic masquerade going on right before our eyes? Aren't you as allergic as I am to the senseless codes these people endorse? In eighteenth-century France, only the very rich had the right to listen to this music. Most often it was actually composed on royal command, just like the plays of Molière. The most powerful families were also the most cultivated ones. And the genre known as "chamber music" was admirably adapted to their needs: they could enjoy it within the walls of their palaces and mansions; usurp art for the benefit of the elite; enclose and privatise cultural production so as to better protect it from the corruption of the *vulgus*. That was how the music we're listening to was appreciated— by the grand ladies of the literary *salons* and their idle friends, beneath chandeliers and gold-leaf painted ceilings, while the great majority of French people lived in crass poverty.

For you, that is secondary: the economic conditions of this music's production belong to the past, whereas the music as art has survived into the present. But don't you think those conditions are present, at least subliminally, in the very notes of *The Goldberg Variations*—their form and structure?

For people who live in the twentieth century, the wish to revive the past is inevitably imbued with aristocratic nostalgia. Whence the term *anachronism*: to play Bach in our day and age—and I would add, especially in conditions identical to those in which he was originally played—is to turn one's back on history, refusing to acknowledge the progress made during the nineteenth and twentieth centuries, shying away from a direct confrontation with the conflicts and contradictions of our times. Only truly "live" music can measure up to the latter challenge; as soon as it is transcribed, it dies and goes over to the reactionary camp, inasmuch as it becomes an indefinitely restorable past.

I don't like to see you this way, subjugated by what you call "great art." I prefer to see you animated, impassioned, talking on the phone or typing something on the typewriter, reacting indignantly to the radio news when we have our morning coffee together… Here, it's as though you'd decided to suspend all your critical faculties. For most other forms of culture—movies, plays, whatever—you manage to keep your distance, as Brecht would say, and filter out the elements of ideology. But wherever music is concerned, your enthusiasm seems to me surprisingly uncritical. In my opinion, ideology is present in music, too—indeed, all the more insidiously in that it is non-verbal. And when you argue in its favour on the basis of "beauty" and "pleasure," how does that differ from petty bourgeois individualism, which tries to convince us that such so-called "pleasures" are strictly a matter of personal taste, rather than a product of the ideological apparatus?

Live music, on the other hand—which in our time means jazz, blues, pop, rock and reggae—really does elicit the pleasure of the masses, while at the same time, in a dialectical movement, it is elicited by this pleasure. Instead of freezing our bodies into anti-erotic rigidity, it loosens up our muscles and stimulates the rhythms of our senses. Instead of stifling and preventing conversation, it provokes it. Do you think it's sheer coincidence that virtually all live music is produced by the oppressed masses of the greatest capitalist power on earth? And always comes into its own precisely during periods of economic crisis? And is now spreading to those countries which are straining under the neocolonialist yoke of the same superpower? How could these facts not have an influence on the music itself?

We go out to listen to Bach, and here we are, nailed to our chairs, lined up in rows like a collection of dead butterflies—whereas when we go to a rock concert the effervescence is immediate—and I so much prefer your body when it throws itself into dancing… Despite all this, I agreed to accompany you here tonight. For me, it's no big thing—I'm capable of self-discipline, and even of using this empty space of time to think about something else. But you shouldn't have dragged Frédéric into it, too. He's fidgeting around on his chair, smoking one cigarette after another—this whole world is just too foreign to him. I don't mean just Bach, I mean the audience's attitude, its passive, neutral receptivity. Remember those nights when he showed us around New Orleans, the fraternity among the Blacks—something we don't often get the chance to observe in France—their bodies swaying all night long to the atavistic rhythms of Black Africa. Everyone called Frédéric "Red" over there, and everyone knew him. Red because he's got reddish hair, as is often the case with mulattos. Frédéric—now, there's an authentic product of the twentieth century for you: a mulatto, a bastard, and all the shrewder for these impurities. Black father with a French name, Dumont, native of New Orleans, sent by the Whites to defend the freedom of other Whites during the Second World War. Fifty percent of the American troops were coloured, whereas Blacks only made up ten percent of the population. Dumont didn't speak a word of French when he disembarked on the Normandy coast, but he fell in love with a local factory girl. Got her pregnant just two days before he was killed by the Krauts. Frédéric, his son, was raised by his mother like a little Frenchman. At the age of twenty, revolted by his country's racist policies in Algeria, adamantly refusing to do his military service under these conditions, he left for the United States. That's when his career took off like a streak of lightning.

You can hear that heroic revolt in his music: his saxophone eloquently denounces the injustice suffered by men of his race in America. Red's blues are a cry of anger, a cry for vengeance—a cry recognized and taken up by oppressed people all over the world. In Harlem, every household has at least one of his records; in Johannesburg, every adolescent who's suffered discrimination can whistle a Frédéric Dumont tune; in all the European capitals, young people flock to hear him. That's because his music is forever young; it needs youthful strength and idealism; it is resolutely on the side of coffee rather than herb tea.

Here, however, we are drowning in herb tea. The ancient values and ancient mores of a crumbling civilisation. A society on the verge of collapse seeking to return to the good old days—what could be more predictable? The renewal of interest in outdated instruments like the harpsichord is but one aspect of this desperate attempt to reverse the course of history and thwart every effort at radical innovation. But the old days were by no means "good." The old days are a corpse no longer capable of hiding its putrefaction. I want for both of us to work towards bringing forth the new days—and to do that, we must desert bedchambers and chamber music; we must be outside, upright, in the street.

Bibi, I can hardly confiscate your Mozart and Mahler records and stow them away in some basement, as was done during the Cultural Revolution in China. All I can do is hope that the different demands of your daily life—our relationship, your job at the paper—will enable you to break the chains that still attach you to the past, one by one. Both the distant and the not-so-distant past: I know your childhood memories and adolescent friendships are an important reason for your stubbornness on this point. But they, too, are anachronisms: I'm sure you'll manage to throw off their dead weight, and become the free and forward-thinking woman I love.

VARIATIO XXIX: GREY

Bibi

...purposely tapping his foot to a different rhythm than the music, just to show his discontent. He'll make sure I realize I've dragged him into the opium den of the bourgeoisie. He'd refuse to acknowledge the beauty of a flower, if it happened to be pinned to the lapel of a businessman. And yet this piece is so very very beautiful. Its wealth is inexhaustible; I could listen to it a thousand times, and each time I would notice something new. I never tire of it—even if it's alienating to take pleasure in passivity. Like watching sports on TV, as Manuel would say. It's true there's a painful contrast between the joy it gives me to listen to music, and my total lack of musical talent. It's always been that way. The school chorus, I would so much have liked to—"Bibi sings off key, she throws us off!"—so I shut up...horribly ashamed. But at least no one prevented me from listening. At fifteen I had a record collection that would have been the envy of many an adult music-lover. The joy of doing my homework while listening to Stravinsky, the joy of getting dressed to Brahms. I didn't yet know all that was part of my bourgeois heritage. Now I'm getting provocative...last week, when I saw a window display at the record store of the complete works of

Mozart, I said to Manuel, "If I had that, I'd become apolitical." He didn't find it very funny. It's what he fears the most: that I might turn my back on the militant discipline he's drilled into me and go sliding back down into the ideological muck from which I came.

Manuel. Manny. My little man. There are a few things that fall outside the little squares of your chart. When you kiss my breasts, should I be thinking about the economic conditions of what is being produced, namely love? You'd like to fit even that into your system: you write about sexuality under capitalism, you analyse misogyny as the offspring of bourgeois values, you make me read Engels's *Origins of the Family* and the contemporary Freudo-Marxists... Manny I wish you would love me with all my awkwardness and all my faults. Stop seeing me as someone to be saved. Stop dragging me to rock concerts... Frédéric couldn't care less about your theories, either, but you never try to convert him—why not? Because he's *making* history, whereas I have to *learn* it...

You don't know what happened. Yes—I like Frédéric's music, too. I went alone to one of his concerts in February, when you were in Brussels for the conference on Power. As usual, I was flabbergasted by his talent, but—maybe because you weren't there, constantly whispering in my ear and tapping your foot... yes, maybe because I was alone—the evening slowly went bad. You know how it is when I start hitting myself over the head. Confronted with that god on stage, I became less than nothing: I started thinking about how I don't know anything, how everything I do is mediocre, writing little articles for a leftist rag… While I go on pursuing my petty little struggles, Frédéric transforms reality before our very eyes, Frédéric brings us happiness here and now, with next to nothing… You get the idea. My mood grew blacker and blacker, and the more people applauded, the more I felt like blowing my brains out. After the concert, Frédéric caught up with me in the street: "Where you goin'? You mad or somethin'? Didn't you like it?" I was surprised he even recognized me, I felt so disfigured by my black thoughts. "Come on, let's have a drink together in my hotel room." I followed him in a state of stupefaction; I don't even know which hotel he was staying at, I think it was somewhere near Opéra. He was incredibly nice to me, he could see I was miserable but he didn't ask any questions. "Sit down," he said, handing me a joint.

I always say no. I'm fed up with saying no. I'm fed up with protecting myself and being afraid. I want to find out what I'm afraid of, what I'm protecting myself from, and for once I said yes.

We shared the joint. Frédéric put on a record by Manu Dibango and went to get his tam-tams. I was a bit hurt that he should abandon me for the music, but at the same time subjugated by the complicated rhythms he was playing, totally effortlessly, and the way his rhythms slid in and out of the recorded music. Maybe I was already stoned. Anyway, it seemed literally miraculous, and again I started grieving over my own musical incompetence. Then the marijuana produced its usual effect: acute paranoia. I felt like an inert heap, sitting in the presence of this sublime guy, this sort of black angel with the magic of music at his fingertips… And then, right away, I reprimanded myself: of course you can do it, stop whining!—and, with a look of distracted delight on my face, I forced myself to drum the arm of the couch with my fingers. Frédéric noticed this, he gave me the tam-tams without a word and went to get his Rwanda drum. I was paralysed before the instrument, I didn't know how to over-come my fear, I said to myself, "Now he'll finally realize how useless I am." With an immense effort, I succeeded in tap-ping on each of the cylinders a couple of times. Frédéric crouched down next to me to show me how it worked: "Listen, Bibi bébé, just let go. Just listen to the music. Can you hear it? Right… Then you go: one, two, three-four. One, two, three-four. That's it." I tried, very conscientious-ly, the way a little girl goes about learning her multiplication tables. I concentrated with all my might but managed less and less easily to hit the beat. Every movement of my hands seemed grotesquely wrong: the music was so beautiful, all I could add to it was ugliness, and that seemed to be the story of my life. I put the tam-tams down and sat there, rigid, on the couch. I didn't want to think about anything, I wanted everything to stop, all motion to cease so I wouldn't have to suffer from my rigidity.

Frédéric got up again, he put his arm around my shoul-ders

he felt the knots in them and massaged my neck

never had I known such patience in the hands of a man

I thought: these are the same fingers that move over the saxophone at the speed of light

I wanted to press up against him, to disappear inside him

he made love to me with so much joy and tenderness I had tears running down my face and he spoke to me the whole time, he said Bibi you're an extraordinary woman, Bibi your breasts are so round, so firm, Bibi your cunt is so warm, so succulent, it drives me nuts, Bibi you can't imagine how good you make me feel

you never speak to me, Manuel

I spent the night in his bed, in his arms, I woke up next to his body, dark brown against the white of the sheet, his skin was very smooth, stretched over the muscles

it had been possible, at last I'd succeeded in letting myself go along with the rhythm, at last at last—

maybe because of the drug? This thought turned me to ice. And then another one, even worse: "It was *last night*." It would never happen again. Frédéric was a great friend of yours, he was always travelling somewhere, it was impossible to be in love with him

he loves countless women, he makes love with countless women, he loves making love, it's public knowledge

everything started falling apart, I thought I'd go crazy, watching him sleep in my arms and thinking there would never again be another night like this one which had been so important to me

this could not have taken place, you had proved it in one of your articles, hadn't you, that good sex is *impossible* under a capitalist regime it had taken place and I had to erase it right away, pretend it hadn't taken place, say nothing about it to you

not because you would have been jealous, no, but because you wouldn't have been jealous, and your lack of jealousy would have denied the importance of what had happened to me

I'd get up and go back to our place and see our walls plastered with posters from all the demonstrations and all the rock concerts we've ever gone to, I'd resume my existence as a tense, anxious, guilt-racked journalist; that very afternoon I had an appointment with a group of women who'd organized a strike at Michelin, and that evening when you returned from Brussels I'd be typing up my article...

That was exactly how things went.

Frédéric phoned to order croissants for our breakfast, and I choked them down. He was gay, humming and doing little dance steps as he made the coffee—but for me, everything I saw was a stillborn memory; I buried it all as I went along.

Frédéric kissed me as I left, a very long kiss, and I was the first to say: See you later.

Later is tonight. Seeing him disturbs me less than I would have thought. Maybe because he arrived late, whereas the invitation specified eight o'clock. Maybe because he finds listening to Bach just as boring as you do, even if the reasons for his boredom aren't the same. I'm seated between the two of you, and it drives me to despair to see that you're managing to spoil my pleasure. But I know it's my own fault; it's because I can't embrace either of your certainties—neither your revolutionary purity and rigour nor his artistic talent.

And how can I expect to impose classical music on you if I don't know how to defend it, either theoretically or practically? I know you'll both be sarcastic afterwards. I know I won't object when you suggest we leave at once to go to the Palace. I know I'll come along with you because I love you both: Manuel the White and Frédéric the Black, I love you from the depths of my grey fog. I love you and I hate you. I'll come along.

VARIATIO XXX: HUNGER

Frédéric Dumont

...sandwiches made for old English ladies without a tooth in their heads, I saw them. They cut off the crust, and between the sheets of cotton batting they spread some unidentifiable substance. And they call that a sandwich! At least in the States people know what a sandwich is. They call them heroes. Huge crusty hunks of bread piled with all sorts of things: ham, cheese, tomato, lettuce, pickle. When you bite into it, you know you're having a meal and not taking communion. God, am I hungry. They've never heard of heroes, here in France. Except the real ones, of course. Can't live without those. "Who's the hero of this play?" they wonder. Is it Monsieur Host? Or Madame Musician? Or Lord Professor So-and-So? Or His Majesty the Editor of *The Day*? The French are still Royalist to the hilt. Every time they have a revolution, a bunch of little princes start hitting each other over the head to see who'll get to be the new king. De Gaulle was the king of kings. Now they're hitting each other over the head to see who's the most Gaullist of them all. Thorer—there's a hero for you. Now his disciples are hitting each other over the head to see who's the best Thorerian. Same goes for Jesus Christ. What do they say? "I'm Daddy's true son!" "No, I am!" "I love my country more than anyone else does!" "No, I do!" "I was chosen by God!" "No, I was!" Everybody needs their daddy.

I wouldn't have minded having one, either. But a real one. Except he happened to be playing the hero and the game turned into real life. Real death. The American cemetery in Normandy is very pretty. Acres and acres of white crosses in tidy rows. Just like in the army: stand in line! Underneath it's a mess of blood and bones, but on top it's all clean and neat. The little heroes of De Gaulle. Thanks, Dad.

I'm a hero, too. The Negro King. The French really get into that. They're proud of me because I'm French and famous. That proves they aren't racist. If I play well, that proves France is a country of great music. If I screw well, that proves France is a country of great lovers. Bunch of shit. Especially because the idea of a Black star makes them horny. Because for them black means forbidden sex. It reminds them of garter belts and Nazi boots and night-time and net-stockings and everything taboo. Look at Madame the Musician's dress, stark black against her white skin—the thrill of Evil. "Look, Mommy! He's black all over!" "Ssshh! Don't point, it's not polite."

You must be white deep down underneath, huh? You're just doing that to get on our nerves. I mean, you could take your skin off and deep down you'd be just like the rest of us. Come on, let's flay you a bit just to see. I mean, it must be depressing to be black like that all the time. That's why you've got the blues, isn't it, you're depressed at being so black

And after all, if we beat you black and blue, a few nice blue bruises wouldn't even show up against your black skin, now would they? Neither would a black eye, huh? If we really want to make sure it hurts, we've got to draw blood

What do you know? It's red...

Red. Red Dumont. The name in lights. Broadway. L.A. Hong Kong. Berlin. Come on, leap a few hurdles, a few borders, prove we're the best. Go sing for France. Go box for Africa. Go play tennis for England. Go play ping-pong for Uncle Sam. Go, Yankees! *Allez, les Verts!* Go, Oppenheimer—with a bit more effort the Americans will have the bomb before the Russians!

Why do I go on? The crowds that flock to hear me. Thunderstorm of applause. From behind the footlights, I can't see a thing. I don't know anyone. I get paid. I get rich. In the States my Brothers keep getting gunned down in the street. Why "my Brothers"? Not because we have the same daddy. The only real brothers are men who have no daddy.

American Blacks eat roots, giblets, dandelions, lard, suspicious kinds of fish, and call it soul food—food for the soul. The Whites find this very poetic; it means Blacks are profound and mysterious and romantic. They go to Black restaurants for their Sunday lunch. They eat soul food and they're real proud of themselves: "So cheap and so delicious!" For the Blacks, it means that since it doesn't nourish the body, it's got to nourish something.

God, am I ever hungry. My stomach is growling. I hope this is almost over.

So then the Blacks start manufacturing heroes, too; little kings. In Africa, in America: "We're the best, we're the beautifulest." No way around it. You'll see, the Central African Republic is on its way to becoming a world power. You'll see, Idi Amin Dada is the emperor of the universe. You'll see, Muhammed Ali can crush any White like an insect. "I'm the biggest, I'm the best!" "No, I am!"

Look, my cock is longer than yours. By a good inch. Oh no, it isn't, that's because you're pulling on it. Look at that guy, he's got one like a bull. Really something! Bah! I've got all of you beat hands down. Not me, you haven't!

Look, our Model Worker laid five thousand and sixty-three bricks in one day!

Look, Madame Dumont sewed thirty-seven pairs of pants!

"I can't do as many as I used to, Frédéric. Before I could do forty, but my eyes aren't so good anymore."

"Why should you want to sew forty pairs of pants instead of thirty-seven, Mama?"

"There's a new girl, real young, you should see her, she's really something, sometimes she does as many as fifty a day!"

"So what's so great about that, Mama? She can't wear fifty pairs of pants at once, can she?"

"You do your job as well as you can, and so do we."

"Hey Red, what's it like being famous?"

"Hey Red, got any gold bricks lying around?"

"Hey Red, whyddaya wanna hang out with us hicks now that you made it?"

Now that I've made it. What exactly have I made? It's like guys who talk about all the women they've "had." What have they had? What have I made ? Dough. Ye-eah.

I never even see it. It's too much fun buying presents. After the concert I'm going to buy something for Bibi. I feel like giving her a thrill. She's wearing her wooden body tonight, as she would say. I'll take them out for dinner in a big brasserie, after these skimpy little appetizers. Manny will splutter for five minutes or so— "You're splurging in one evening what an unskilled worker earns in a month!"—but eventually he'll shut up. The sauerkraut going in will prevent the bullshit from coming out. And we'll wash it down with some Alsatian wine—

"Mama, what can I buy for you?"

"Nothing, dear, I don't need anything."

"Mama, I want to give you a present. It's not a question of need, what do you want?"

"Oh, nothing, you should put your money in the bank, you never know. I'm happy just as I am."

She's happy, for Christ's sake. All she's got to do is slug it out for two more years until retirement, that's why she's happy.

"Mama, when you retire, we'll go to the Côte d'Azur and buy ourselves a beautiful house by the sea. You'll be warm for the first time in your life."

"I like it fine here; it's all I know. Travelling is for you."

London. Frankfurt. New Orleans. Rio. Sydney. Niamey. Tokyo. Different concert halls, different airplanes, different women, different hotel rooms; only my cock and my saxophone stay the same. So why do I go on?

"What makes Frédéric Dumont run?" A whole page in *The Day*. The story of my life. How I found my roots in the States. How I started playing when I discovered the blues—I had them in my blood because of my daddy. Bunch of shit. The only thing I learned in the States is that there's no such thing as roots. That we're nothing but four billion zombies looking for our roots. That people with roots are often mean and dangerous. The blues is the only way I know of saying these things. The blues let me talk to everybody. But I ain't got them in my blood. Communion makes my stomach turn. "This is my body, this is my blood." That's cannibalism, man. Same goes for "This is my blues." The hungry crowds devouring me. They need soul food because they're already stuffed to the gills with body food. Meanwhile the other crowds, the ones who never come to my concerts, are still starving to death. The whole thing stinks.

Still, I'm the one who's hungry tonight. It's past nine-thirty already. Everybody's starting to cast furtive glances at the balcony, to make sure their little white sandwiches haven't gone fluttering away like so many butterflies.

Hey, the moon's come up—a full moon. Bet that was calculated in advance. The black magic of the white lady. She's thinking the same thing I am. That maybe tonight the magic's going to work; that maybe the music will finally bring people together. Could happen…you never know. Once in a blue moon, as the Americans like to say. Which means: never.

Are you just about done, Madame Musician? I could eat a horse.

ARIA: BASSO CONTINUO

Liliane Kulainn

They recognize the theme: it's returned at last. I don't need the little black spots anymore; Adrienne can take a rest; there are no more pages to turn. All of us will be relieved. We will have done our duty. We will have accomplished something this evening. We'll be able to say that instead of having read a book or gone to the movies, we attended a concert. Or gave one, as the case may be. We will have had the patience and the civility to hold out to the end. We will have heard all the variations, in their invariable order. No one will have burst into tears or laughter, no one will have uttered any oaths or obscenities. We can be proud of ourselves.

I don't need to pay attention to my little sausages anymore. They'll be able to make it by themselves, I can trust them now. The brain will go on discreetly, mechanically emitting its signals, and the arms will go on transmitting them. My back aches. There's a bad pain in both my back and shoulders. And I don't have the right to rub them or go off to bed—not yet. Almost, but not yet. The constraint continues, catastrophe is still possible—up to the very last. This must never be forgotten.

Did I play well? I have no idea. The notes came. I drew them from the instrument, one after the other, I allowed them to come, trying not to do them too much violence. And when they came, they carried with them an entire universe: not only Bach but a whole series of composers; not only Goldberg but a whole crowd of insomniacs; not only the eighteenth century but all the ages past and yet to come. I was afraid, at times, as I juggled with all of this, that I wouldn't be able to control it—perhaps it was stronger than I was? I was afraid I might let the whole thing drop. But I wanted to take the risk.

The audience is made up of people I have loved and people I still love. I wanted them to allow me to take this risk, for the time being. Yes, for the being of time. They allowed it. In coming to the concert, they came to my assistance. They *helped* me, and I'm grateful. That is all. As people say after an evening of intense conversation: of course, we haven't solved the world's problems, but—

But. I'm not unhappy with the way this ritual has unfolded. It's allowed me to understand a few things. Not people, but things about people. Which is something. It's not everything, but it's something. Everything or nothing is a false dilemma. Just like the door that must be open or closed.— Just like the pianoforte, too, as opposed to the ideal instrument. I'd succeeded in reducing the dynamic possibilities of music by switching from the piano to the harpsichord. And I wanted something narrower still. I wanted the melodic range to shrink as well, to close in around me. The E: *do, re, mi*. An instrument that would play nothing but me's. Me and nobody else.

It's true that all of this was imagined by me. But there's no such thing as a me that's *only* me. I'm the one who composed every single variation. Using the notes of Bach. Using the people in this room. All in my head. I'm sure I got a few things wrong. In fact, my ideas were pretty vague when I set out. I wasn't even sure who knew whom, what had happened first and what came later, how the different events would intertwine… I *pretended* to be speaking for thirty people. Not in the French sense of the word, as pretention, but in the English sense, as make-believe. It seemed to me I distinctly heard two or three false notes—my fingers must have slipped, and I was afraid this might cause the entire chandelier to smash to the floor. But I could sense very strongly that the moon was rising in the sky; so there was no doubt but that time was passing, and that all of us were still here getting older together. I went on. They allowed me to go on. At most I would hear a sigh now and then—and, in the background, the sound of Paris traffic. For me, that was part of the concert: I've never once played in this room without hearing the city outside. Bach never composed in total silence, either.

It's true my back aches dreadfully. But I feel different. Towards the middle of the performance, imperceptibly, the meaning of the concert itself began to change. Here and there—just fleeting moments, but nonetheless—I got the impression I was actually hearing the music. *The music I was playing.* That's something that had never happened to me before. There would be fragments of sound, modulations—it was happening both inside my body and in the air around me—music! It made me very joyful. This is something I could never admit to the others—that up until now, I'd never heard the music. How beautiful it is! How come everyone else knew about it before I did?

I can feel that the instrument is aching, too. When you play the harpsichord for a long stretch at a time, the notes very gradually go flat. The high notes suffer sooner than the low ones: they're attached to shorter strings, and when the strings get stretched so much as a millimeter, you can tell the difference. This probably isn't audible to everyone, but I can hear it. I handled the notes a bit roughly in some of the variations, to get what I needed out of them—my own violence surprised me. They have good reason to be exhausted, and so do I. For the moment, I'm still attuned to my instrument.

As things have turned out, it was not an instrument of torture.

The wheel has gone through a complete revolution and I've emerged unscathed. A few cramps—a small price to pay for the understanding that's been bestowed upon me. A midsummer night's dream, as I said to Bernald—but, quite unexpectedly, the spell was cast on me. It will be lifted, shortly. But though dream-images dissolve upon awakening, they never disappear completely. They remain in the air, like the fragments of music I heard. I'll be able to return to them. Or not return to them. I will have brought them to life for a while; I'll be able to bring them to life again. Or bring other ones to life. One night you need Bach, and one night you need sleep. "One night" does not exist. It is merely something between everything and nothing.

I can hear fidgeting in the audience. Just the first stirrings. People are getting ready to wake up. Some of them will have had lovely dreams and others nightmares. All of them can sense the end approaching. And all of them suspect that in reality, Time does not exist; that there are any number of times; and that each of them has an end. Which is why they're ill at ease. They squirm around on their chairs, in their beds, in their bodies, each of them watching the others to see if they've reached the same conclusion. Now they're going to have to move on to something different. Change rituals. Change registers. Pull a different stop. Teach someone else how to go play the harpsichord, uncork a bottle of champagne, talk, love, cease to talk and cease to love. Some day, I'll stop playing the harpsichord. I know that. But not yet. I've only just heard its music for the first time! I find it marvellous, and I'm so very happy…

My thinking more and more resembles that of a child. I'm stammering, repeating myself, no longer sure of what I'm trying to say. Because I'm tired. But that's what *The Goldberg Variations* are for; it's fine to feel tired when they come to an end. I've always been afraid of fatigue, but this evening I'm finally enjoying it. When I stop, I don't know if it will be to wake up or fall asleep. Music is somewhere in between. In fact, I don't know if I *will* stop… Perhaps I'll start over again immediately, with the Variatio I. Just when they think we've got nothing more to say, we could pull a stunt like that on them, eh, my little harpsichord? What do you say? Shall we give the wheel another spin? Go all the way around again? Maybe the stories we'd tell would be completely different. In fact I'm sure they would. But no—it's wonderful to stop, too. I agree with you. Both of us will heave a deep sigh. That's enough for tonight; yes it's the end now.